LEVI'S VOW

PENNY ZELLER

Dedicated to America's farmers who work hard to ensure we have food on our tables each day.

CHAPTER ONE
IDAHO TERRITORY, 1880

NORAH WROTE THE DETAILS on the blackboard just inside the door at Winrow's Mercantile, placed the chalk on the ledge, then stood back to peruse her slanted handwriting. *Hired hand needed. Inquire at the Hammett farm two miles west of town.*

She tilted her head to one side and debated removing it. After all, it had been Mama's idea to post the request. Had Norah had her own way, she'd have forged ahead as things were and not given a second thought to again requesting help.

Such a request hadn't been effective last time, and it wasn't likely to succeed this time.

So deep in her thoughts, Norah jumped when she heard someone behind her. Cautiously, she turned and came face-to-face with a man she'd never seen before. With narrowed eyes, gritted teeth, and fists clenched at his sides, he reminded her of an angry bull about to stomp before charging.

The man's proximity was far too close, and Norah backed herself against the blackboard.

He followed and stood within inches of her with his thick arms crossed. An unkempt beard covered most of his face, and a muscle beneath his right eye twitched. "Erase it," he growled.

Now wasn't the time to freeze and show fear, but she couldn't stop the icy emotions from taking root in her heart. Norah scanned the room, but the one other customer paid her no mind. Mrs. Winrow must have slipped into the backroom, for she was nowhere to be seen. A fresh rush of foreboding jolted through her, and she worried she may lose the noonday meal she'd eaten mere hours ago. "I—I beg your pardon?"

The man gripped her arm, causing her to wince. "You heard me, woman. Erase it." His breath carried the foul odor of whiskey mixed with bacon. Norah fought the bile rising in her throat due to the stench of his breath and the fear that engulfed her. He grabbed the wool eraser and tapped her hand with it. "You heard what I said."

She reluctantly took the eraser from him, and he released her arm but maintained his position.

"Why?" Her voice squeaked and she hated that she sounded scared. "Why when I am in need of a hired hand for my farm?"

Instead of answering, the man reached toward her. She flinched, but instead of striking her, he pounded on the blackboard with his fist, causing it to rattle against the wood on which it hung. "Don't you even think about writin' it again. And don't you tell no one neither. Things won't go well for you if you do. Now erase it," he hissed.

Keeping an eye on the man, Norah removed the handwriting. The man glowered at her, then turned on his heel and stomped from the mercantile.

Norah's breath heaved, and she closed her eyes, reeling from the confrontation. Her heart raced as dizziness swirled through her, and she gripped a nearby shelf to steady herself.

The questions loomed. Why would someone threaten her for writing an advertisement seeking help? What would the man do if she did tell the sheriff?

Praying for calm, Norah bit her lip and willed her heartbeat to slow. Mama and the children were waiting on her. She couldn't stay backed against the blackboard forever.

Forcing herself to proceed with the other reason she'd traveled to town, Norah willed her weakened legs to obey her command to peruse the store and gather the needed provisions.

For a moment, she failed to recall the final item on Mama's list. *Baking powder.* Yes, that was it. She found the four items and placed them on the counter.

"How are you today, Norah?" Mrs. Winrow asked.

"Fine, thank you."

But she wasn't fine. What if she encountered the man again? What if he waited for her outside? Followed her home?

Don't allow your mind to wander in such a way. God will protect you.

He would, wouldn't He? She had to believe God would keep her safe. Safe for her children. Safe for Mama. They needed her.

Mrs. Winrow's brow furrowed. "You're rather pale. Are you not feeling well?"

"Just a lot of burdens lately. That's why Mama and I decided to find a hired hand to help us with the farm." Her voice shook. Would Mrs. Winrow notice?

The kind woman shook her graying head. "Just hoping he doesn't turn out like that last man you had."

"Me too."

That was one reason why Norah hadn't wanted to advertise for help. She didn't need a repeat of what happened with the prior hired hand.

She couldn't afford it. Not emotionally. And not financially.

"I'll certainly keep an ear out for someone needing a job."

Even as Mrs. Winrow said it, Norah doubted many would step forward. For one, they remembered the past all too well. And for two, most able-bodied men already worked on Payne Deaton's sizable farm. She couldn't pay anywhere near the wages he did.

As if Mrs. Winrow read Norah's thoughts, she added, "We do get some drifters from time to time. Perhaps one of them will be seeking employment."

Norah offered a weak smile. Mrs. Winrow and her husband hadn't judged Norah for what had happened two years ago, unlike some in town. "I appreciate that. Thank you."

"Yes, dear. And I'll just put these items on your account."

Norah exhaled a sigh of relief that the owner of the store would add the items to her already-excessive bill. She hadn't the money for the necessities today. Wouldn't have it until the crop came in.

If there even was a crop this year.

The fetid combination of urine mixed with body odor and perspiration was a combination he'd not soon forget.

"You're more antsy than a rabbit being preyed upon by a coyote. Ain't you gonna be here a bit?"

Levi Callahan blew out a deep breath and regarded Kuntz, the man in the neighboring jail cell. "I'm not supposed to be here at all," he muttered.

Kuntz released an obnoxious chortle that echoed throughout the sheriff's office. "That's what they all say. Trust me. I'm here every week, and I done heard that same thing about five dozen times." He offered a sharp, nasally snort, followed by expectorating onto the cell floor. "I seen drunks, horse thieves, murderers, you name it. I seen it all."

But Levi was different. He never imbibed, didn't steal horses, and wasn't a murderer. Instead, he'd saved someone from one who could be a potential murderer, given the man continued in his cruel ways. Mrs. Shipley's bruised face entered his mind unannounced. Levi shoved the image aside and stared at the drunkard gripping the bars separating their cells. "I'm not anything like them," he said.

Kuntz shrugged and plopped on his cot. "Ain't no one in this town of a hunnerd people believes that. Especially not me."

Levi ignored that dismal fact and averted his attention to the tiny barred window. Across the street, Criselda spoke to Mrs. Hansen's daughter, prattling on as though she hadn't just broken hers and Levi's engagement four days ago.

Mrs. Hansen said something to her daughter, then walked across the street and entered the sheriff's office. She held two steaming bowls in her hand, likely bean soup, the fare Levi had been served for every meal since he'd been arrested.

The sheriff opened the cell door, and Mrs. Hansen handed Levi the smaller of the two bowls. Hardly enough to feed a child, let alone a full-grown man. It amazed Levi that, if he was such a dangerous threat, why did the sheriff allow Mrs. Hansen to hand him the bowl?

"Thank you, ma'am."

Mrs. Hansen said nothing, only avoided his gaze.

She was Ma's best friend. He'd known her since he was just a young'un, but she was just like most, if not all, of the town's residents—she wanted nothing to do with him as of last Saturday night.

The incident that altered Levi's life forever.

The sheriff locked the cell again, and Mrs. Hansen repeated the food delivery to Kuntz.

"Thank you. I be appreciatin' the soup," he said.

Mrs. Hansen offered a slight grin "You're welcome. Glad you enjoy it."

Kuntz didn't bother to pray before he slurped his soup all in one gulp. Levi nearly gagged at the obnoxious sound, and he considered himself one with a strong constitution.

The sheriff placed his hat on his head and said he'd be back soon. Levi took a seat on the cot and rationed his bean soup, noting that just during his time in jail, he'd lost weight and strength. Nothing that some hard work on the farm wouldn't cure, but disturbing all the same.

Kuntz rattled the bars. "If you ain't gonna eat that, I will."

Levi ignored him and figured he could count the number of beans in the paltry soup.

The sheriff returned an hour later and unlocked Levi's cell. "You're free to go." His words failed to resonate at first.

"Free to go?"

His dismissive wave ushering Levi from the cell confirmed his words.

Kuntz gripped the bars of his own cell. "If yer gonna complain, I'll trade you places."

Levi didn't need any further urging. "I'm not complaining. Just wondering...do I need to return to appear before a judge?"

The sheriff led him to the front door. "Apparently, Mrs. Shipley verified your story."

His jaw went slack. Why had she waited nearly a week to do so?

"She's on her way back East to live with her family."

Questions swarmed through his mind, but for now, Levi would be grateful for the opportunity to clear his name. To restore his reputation. To return to farming the land.

Levi walked the two miles home, eager to share with his parents the good news. He passed three people on his way, all of whom he'd known his entire life. None of whom acknowledged him. Would they change their minds once they discovered the error of his arrest? Would Criselda realize she wanted to resume courting him?

What would Pa say when he arrived at the farm?

Rather than go to the bunkhouse first, Levi instead ambled up the stairs of the home his parents rented from the farm's owner. He was anxious to share with his family about his release and eager to return to the life he knew before that fateful night.

The aroma of pot roast lingered in the air beyond the front door, and his stomach growled. He couldn't wait for something other than runny bean soup for every meal.

Levi opened the door to see his family sitting at the supper table. Pa abruptly stood, his hasty action causing his chair to fall backwards and crash against the floor. He pointed a finger at Levi. "What are you doing here, boy?"

Never "Levi". Never "son" . Always "boy". He would be twenty-nine soon. Hardly a boy. Did Pa even know he had a name?

"They released me. Mrs. Shipley came forward and told the sheriff what happened."

Ma's eyes rounded. His younger brother, Jay, focused on his meal and moved a piece of roast from one side of the plate to the other. And Pa stormed toward him. "You ain't welcome here."

"But, Pa, like I said, they released me. The law made a mistake in arresting me, and now I'm a free man."

"Ain't nothing you can do to remedy a tarnished reputation. You've brought shame on the Callahan family. Shame that ain't never gonna be forgiven."

Pa's thundering voice boomed throughout the room, causing Levi's stomach to bunch into a knot as if someone had punched him in the gut. As hungry as he'd been five minutes ago, he knew now he wouldn't be able to eat a thing. Pot roast or not.

"They mistakenly arrested me. I was defending Mrs. Shipley."

His father took three giant paces toward him and invaded Levi's space. Pa's breath wreaked of stale onions, and Levi resisted the urge to take a step back to escape the odor.

Pa jabbed a finger into Levi's delicate shoulder flesh. "You crossed Mr. Shipley. The man who rents us this land. The man I work for." The seething words accompanied several curses, indicating Pa's opinion of Levi. "You are no longer welcome in this home."

"But, Pa... Ma?"

Ma said nothing, only fiddled with her napkin. His brother slunk lower in his seat.

"Fetch your stuff from the bunkhouse and be on your way. Don't darken our door ever again." Pa scowled at him, sparks of rage igniting in his eyes. "You've always been a worthless sort. Why can't you be more like your younger brother?" Pa shoved him hard, causing Levi to nearly lose his footing. "Now git, boy. Git your horse and ride on out of here. Don't care where you go. Just don't come back."

"Please, allow me to explain."

"You ain't no son of mine."

Pa's words shook Levi, and the emotion just beneath the surface crushed him. Anger meshed with frustration and pain. It was no use arguing with Pa. He'd never relent. It was pointless begging him to reconsider—to rethink disowning his oldest son.

Levi grit his teeth and offered a clipped nod. "Goodbye, Ma. Goodbye, Jay."

Ma simply nodded, and Jay dropped his chin to his chest. No one dared cross Pa.

"And one other thing…" Pa's eyes narrowed. "Don't be thinkin' you're gonna be sleeping in the bunkhouse or the barn or under the stars on this property. You find somewhere else to rest your head tonight and every night after that."

Acid sloshed a blistering trail in his throat, and Levi trudged out the door, back down the steps, and toward the bunkhouse. He ground back the sting of tears. Showing any weakness would only validate Pa's opinion of Levi's worthlessness.

Pa despised weakness, and tears in particular.

Being in jail tonight would be preferable to being homeless.

At least he still had his horse, Eagle, and some meager possessions. He burrowed through his belongings in the bunkhouse he shared with Jay. A pair of trousers, a shirt, and coat, a pair of socks, his dark-brown Stetson, Bible, rifle, and Colt revolver.

He caught a glimpse of the acreage through the bunkhouse window. Levi had once dreamed of owning his own home. Building it with his own hands. Sharing it with a wife and children.

Criselda.

But she'd spurned him with some haughty words spoken in front of the sheriff, his deputy, and Kuntz. Words Levi thought he'd never hear a woman like her speak.

There would be no constructing a house, marrying Criselda, and starting a family with her.

Levi yanked the nearly threadbare blanket from his bed, threw his trousers, shirt, and socks in it, and created a bedroll. He tucked his Colt into its holster, put his knife in his trouser pocket, and removed his rifle from the hooks on the wall.

Then he took one final perusal of the room in an attempt to commit to memory the past eight years of sharing it with Jay.

When he emerged from the bunkhouse, he noticed Pa standing on the porch of the house, arms folded across his chest. Without so much as a wave, Levi proceeded to the barn, saddled Eagle, mounted, and rode west to...

Where?

Tonight he'd find somewhere to lay his head, and in the morning, he'd figure out where to go.

CHAPTER TWO

LEVI RODE FOR THE next two days, stopping only to water his horse, eat, and sleep. It was as though he couldn't get far enough away from the town and the people who turned their backs on him.

On the third day just as the sun was setting, he entered a small town with five buildings—two saloons, a dry goods store, a livery, and a blacksmith. He stopped at the dry goods store, tethered his horse, and entered the only building in town that appeared somewhat tidy. In less than five minutes, he learned there were no jobs to be had. Attempting not to be discouraged, Levi mounted his horse and continued through town.

At the far edge, three men were tossing a wallet amongst them, keeping it away from a short, gray-haired man who attempted to jump up and intercept it before the next man caught it.

He failed miserably.

Levi wrestled with what to do. On one hand, the matter didn't pertain to him, and he knew what happened last time he intruded on something that was none of his concern. On the other, the desperation in the elderly man's actions prompted him to stop and help.

The latter choice won.

He again tethered his horse and strolled toward the group of men. "Is there a problem?"

The largest of the three, with a belly that hung over his belt, glared at him. "Who's asking?"

"I am."

A man with short, curly black hair spoke next. "What are you? The law?" He slapped his thigh and chortled, his raucous voice carrying through the vacant street. "Oh, that's right. This town don't got no lawmen."

A third man, a puny, balding fellow, held the wallet to his chest. "Guess we better git on anyhow. The saloon is beckoning us."

The older man stepped toward him. "Can I have my wallet back first?"

"Can you have your wallet back?" The large one shook his head. "No."

Levi took a step closer. "If it's his wallet, why would you keep it?"

"Do we need to teach you a lesson for sticking your nose where it don't belong?" The man with the curly hair rested his hand on his revolver.

"I'm not looking for trouble, gentleman, but this man needs his wallet back."

Puny growled. "What are you? His grandson?"

The desperation in the elderly man's eyes tugged at Levi. "Yes, I am. Grandpa, how do you always manage to get yourself into these situations?"

The elderly man shrugged. "Sorry, Grandson. I didn't mean for this to happen—just wanted to purchase some supplies."

Curly Hair sneered, revealing plentiful gums, but few teeth. "Give him the wallet. He ain't worth it."

Puny threw the wallet at the old man, hitting him in the side of the head. "Grandpa" stooped, retrieved it, and stuffed it into his pocket. "Pleasure spending time with you, but I best be on my way. Come on, Grandson. We got miles to go before the day is over."

Five minutes later, Levi and the man rode out of town and toward the hills. "Name's Elmer Neeley. Much obliged for your help back there. I need my wallet if I'm to make it to Nevada. You headed that way as well?"

"I'm Levi Callahan, and no, sir. I'm not sure where I'm headed, but I aim to stay in the Idaho Territory."

They rode until they arrived at a grove of trees. "Well, Grandson, this looks as good a place as any to bed down for the night."

Levi chuckled at Elmer's statement. "Sounds good to me, Grandpa."

Elmer gathered some wood for a fire. "So, what are you running from?"

"Who says I'm running from something?"

"It's as clear as the nose on your face, my boy."

"Just looking for honest work." Levi hauled over two tree stumps for seats, and unrolled his bedroll. "Are you familiar with this area?"

"Not so much. I'm from the northern part of the territory, but my sister wants me to visit her and her family in Nevada." Elmer shrugged. "Got nothing better to do, so I agreed. So you want to farm?"

"I do."

"Have experience?"

"On the farm I worked with my pa and brother back home." The thought of Pa left a sour taste in his mouth. Pa had always been a hard man, but Levi never figured he'd disown his own son.

Elmer scratched his head. "Then why aren't you still working with your pa—if you don't mind me asking?"

Levi did mind because he wasn't the type to share his woes with anyone, but there was something about Elmer Neely that indicated trustworthiness. Besides, it wasn't like the man would ever meet Levi's family. "I'm no longer welcome at my parents' home."

"Ah. I see. Your pa a difficult man?"

"He is."

They ate before Elmer unpacked a worn Bible from his saddle bag. "Gonna spend some time with the Lord before we get some shuteye." He flipped through the pages, leaned forward towards the glow of the fire, and studied the Word of God.

Levi hadn't read the Bible for some time. As a young'un, Ma took him and his brother to church on occasion—never with Pa.

Elmer lowered the Bible. "You know the Lord?"

"Somewhat."

"Either you do or you don't. Ain't no somewhat about it."

"I used to think He was harsh and unloving like my Pa."

"And now?"

Levi stroked the beginnings of a beard. "I know He sent Jesus to die for our sins, so that shows me He's a loving God. But I do wonder if He ever gives up on us when we fail."

"He is a loving God. A God of justice too. But He is slow to anger. I was just reading for the hundredth time in Exodus 34:6 about how He's merciful, gracious, longsuffering, and abundant in goodness and truth."

That night when he should have been sleeping, Levi ruminated on all he and Elmer discussed. He propped his hands behind his head and stared at the starry sky. Stars placed one-by-one by a Creator who actually cared for him. Loved him. Sent His Son to die for him. Elmer had patiently answered all of Levi's questions—and there were many—until the old man nodded off.

A newfound wonder at having a Father who would never abandon and reject him brought about a recently-discovered joy Levi had never before experienced. His earthly father may turn his back on him, but Levi's Heavenly Father never would.

⸎

Norah placed the crate of goods into the back of the wagon next to the larger crate Mr. Winrow had carried out for her. It was then that she saw a tattered piece of stationery kept in place by a small rock.

Hand trembling, she retrieved the note, written with a haphazard hand and atrocious spelling, and scanned it.

Watch yer back.

She stared at the soiled white paper and handwriting that pressed through to the other side.

Norah's heart pounded, and her legs threatened to give way.

Why was someone so bent on removing her from the place she'd called home for the past several years?

"Mrs. Hammett, are you all right?"

She turned to see Mr. Winrow standing in the mercantile's doorway. Should she make mention of the note? She thought of the man she'd encountered and his threat and decided better of it. "Yes, Mr. Winrow, I'm fine."

One lie to save a life was all right, wasn't it?

"All right, then. Have a good evening and be sure to tell your ma the missus and I said 'hello'."

"I will." Norah didn't dare say more. If she did, Mr. Winrow would for certain hear the quiver in her voice.

Had the same man who insisted she erase the advertisement also leave the note in her wagon? She suppressed a shiver as worry rippled through her. *Lord, please keep us safe. We're just now able to find our way without Douglas.*

Should she tell Sheriff Perez? The man was new to town so she hadn't spoken more than a few words to him at church, but perhaps he could alleviate her fears.

After a brief moment of hesitation, Norah walked toward the sheriff's office, her mind reeling. Hadn't enough chaos happened in her life in the past few years? She turned the corner into the small wooden structure that housed the jail and the sheriff's office, and she poked her head in the doorway. "Sheriff?"

No answer.

The sheriff's chair was empty, as was the jail. If she delayed in town much longer, she'd not make it home before dark.

Yet if she allowed whoever was threatening her to get away with this...

Norah rushed down the boardwalk toward the wagon. Dark clouds mushroomed across the sky and the scent of rain filled her nostrils. If she was to avoid the impending storm and make it home before nightfall, Norah ought to leave town as soon as possible. She secured her shawl more tightly around her shoulders, hoping to somehow keep out the sudden chill and the sense of foreboding.

A few moments later, Norah beckoned the horses toward home. Her mind, as it did on occasion, reverted to Douglas. Had he not done what he did, she wouldn't be in desperate straits seeking a hired hand.

The buildings soon became sparser as Norah traveled toward home. Trees with their new spring leaves blew in the wind, and a raindrop pelted the buckboard beside her. The deeply-rutted road jostled her to and fro as she passed by a few houses surrounded by freshly-tilled fields.

With the exception of her early childhood years, Norah had always resided in the Idaho Territory and had grown to appreciate the mountains in the distance, the spring wildflowers, perfect summers, and the numerous farms dotting the landscape. When she and Mama left Boise City by stagecoach and traveled to Cuyler Junction at the request of Doc, whom Mama had known during her own childhood, Norah's love for the area increased.

Soon after she and Mama arrived, she met Douglas, a handsome young man with a charming personality. They married after a whirlwind courtship and welcomed their son a year later and a daughter two years after that. They purchased their own farm, and Douglas attempted to farm the land. But even early in their marriage, she sensed his lack of motivation, combined with restlessness and an impatience for more than a farm in disrepair from the former owner's neglect. Drought and an early freeze prevented a bountiful harvest during the first couple of years, but they managed to recover, and with Mama residing with them, Norah was able to work alongside Douglas in the fields.

When he didn't devise excuses to avoid doing the work that had become mundane to him.

Norah recalled the regret so prevalent in his countenance when he returned home after a tiresome day working the soil. Another day attempting to support a family when he'd rather be seeking adventure.

While she'd prayed constantly for her marriage and for Douglas to love her and the children and find contentment on the farm, those prayers had gone unanswered.

Two years later, she continued to struggle in a cloak of sorrow and anger as she sought to forgive the one who had deemed her unworthy. A man who had secretly found love in the arms of a woman from an affluent Cuyler Junction family.

Deep in thought, Norah jumped at the muffled sound of a man's voice competing with the wind.

"Well, hello, Norah. A fine day for a trip to town now, isn't it?"

She swiveled to see Payne Deaton in his buggy beside her. Norah slowed the horses to a stop, and Payne did the same.

"Yes, it is."

Payne removed his black top hat. "My dear lady, I once again wish to convey to you my desire to purchase your farm. I know that without your husband, managing such a generous portion of Idaho's landscape has been tedious to say the least."

Tedious accurately described the struggle, but Norah had never been one to concede when life became unmanageable. Had she been that type of woman, she and Mama would have never made it on their own all those years.

"I appreciate your earnestness in attempting to persuade me to sell you my property, but once again, I am uninterested."

A frown breached Payne's mouth before he recovered and again offered a broad smile. "You would no longer have to concern yourself with the banknote. Mr. Shreffler indicated you are behind in your payments."

The banker ought to have kept such insinuations to himself, but Norah didn't mention that. "I best be on my way."

"You do realize you are in desperate straits if you don't have an abundant crop this year, and frankly, what with the loss of your hired hand and just you and your aging mother to operate it, your chances of success are nil."

Mama would *not* appreciate being referred to as "aging". At forty-eight, she could hardly be considered elderly. Payne's expectant and prideful expression drew Norah back to a time when she'd thought the man to be an upstanding and somewhat dapper gentleman. Once after she and Mama arrived home from church with the children, Norah had accepted a ride in his expensive buggy to take a tour of Payne's acreage.

Such a fool she'd been.

Or perhaps, in the grief of losing a husband to another woman and then subsequently to the silver mines, Payne's interest proved she was still worthy of a man's attention.

Yes, Payne's congeniality towards her, his seemingly honorable reputation, steady church attendance, and his well-bred educated vernacular should have proven him a fine catch.

But something had led her to re-evaluate her first impression of Payne. Something she couldn't explain. Something before she'd discovered his sister, Bridget's, fondness for Douglas.

"I will have to decline your offer once again, Payne."

"Again? Now, Norah, I know you're a wise woman."

"Mama and I are contemplating hiring a hand to assist us with the crops this year." *Hopefully, one who does not determine to steal from us.*

Had she not been paying attention, she would have missed the brief narrowing of Payne's eyes. Something about him frightened her for the first time.

"I'm shocked at your revelation, Norah. Do you not recall the last hand you hired? A bad judge of character on your part, to say the least." He smiled at her, as if his words could be softened by doing so.

How could she not remember the last and only hired hand? She'd not even wanted to advertise for another one, but she and Mama were desperate. For if the farm failed, where else could they go? Not even the measly amount of money Payne had offered several months ago for her farm would get them very far into a new life after they paid the bank what was owed.

The rain fell at a steady pace now, and her hair whipped around her ears. Payne remained safely sheltered beneath the roof of the buggy, undeterred by the storm. "I need to get home. Perhaps we can continue this conversation another time." Thankfully, her voice sounded stronger than she felt.

"I understand your need to return home before nightfall. Please consider my offer. Despite what some of the townsfolk say, I do believe you do possess some wisdom about you. Good day, Norah." He tipped his hat and vanished as quickly as he had arrived.

Norah's breath caught. Yes, she knew some of the hateful words a few in Cuyler Falls had said since Douglas had publicly divorced her and then hastily left to seek his adventure. The words still hurt, even two years later. Perhaps they always would.

Anxiety from the encounter in the mercantile, the note in her wagon, and seeing Payne overwhelmed her, and Norah begged her heartbeat to return to normal.

CHAPTER THREE

CHURCH ON SUNDAY WAS a welcome reprieve from the dilemmas and obstacles that plagued her.

"Ma, do I have to eat my oatmeal?" Hazel blanched and pushed the mush aside. "I haven't ever liked it."

Mama laughed. "You're only four, Hazel. Perhaps you'll grow to like it someday."

"Sorry, Grandma, but I don't think so." She pointed to her older brother. "Look, Enoch doesn't like it either."

Enoch swirled the oatmeal around with a spoon in one hand and rested his head in the other.

"We'll be late for church if we don't hurry." Norah fashioned her hair into a bun, bemoaning the stubborn strand that refused to cooperate.

"I don't want to be late for church," Hazel chirped.

Enoch glanced up at Hazel, then returned his attention to his uneaten breakfast. Of all of them, her young son had taken Douglas's leaving the hardest. If Norah could take his pain upon herself, she would.

Norah put an arm around him and tugged him to her. Enoch peered up at her with doleful eyes. "I'm not hungry, Ma," he said, his voice barely above a whisper.

She'd only be grateful he spoke. "Please try to eat as much as you can or you'll be hungry during church. It'll be a while before we eat again." Enoch's reasons for not eating breakfast sharply contrasted Hazel's. Enoch didn't eat because melancholy still lingered. Hazel didn't eat because she was a particular sort. Unfortunately, neither excuse proved worthwhile because food couldn't be wasted.

The pouring rain and the horses clopping through the mud created a messy journey to church. Norah proceeded along the road, dodging puddles as best as she could. She and Mama rushed the children into the church, but on Norah's way inside, she noticed an unwelcome face lurking in the trees, his broad-brimmed cowboy hat deflecting the rain.

The man who'd threatened her.

Norah inhaled a sharp breath and returned her focus to getting inside the church. Fears clouded her mind, and she instinctively watched the church's door should the man enter. Doc arrived seconds after they did and immediately took his place beside Mama in the pew where they always sat.

Norah leaned across Mama. "Doc?"

"Good morning, Norah." Doc smiled, but his attention was on Mama.

"Did you happen to see a man standing outside? A man other than the men in here?"

"I didn't. Is everything all right?"

As much as she thought of Doc as the godly father she'd never had, Norah wasn't sure telling him the details was wise, for what could he do?

"Has anyone seen the Perez family?" she asked.

Mama peeked behind them. "I don't believe they are here today."

The man's threats caused an uptick in her heartbeat. It was just as well Sheriff Perez wasn't in attendance today since she wavered between whether or not to tell him about the incidents.

Doc gazed lovingly at Mama, taking in every word she said as she told him one of Hazel's antics. One would have to be blind, or at the very least unaware, to not notice Doc's genuine interest. He and Mama had known each other during their school days in Boise City, then had gone separate ways—Mama to marry Pa, and Doc to attend medical school—then found each other again. Norah suspected Mama had reasons for declining Doc's offer of marriage. Truth be told, she wasn't sure what she'd do if she didn't have Mama's help.

Reverend Svensen led the prayer before they sang, and when they took their seats again, Norah perused the humble church. Bridget Deaton's eyes bored into her, a scowl on the woman's face.

At least there was a modicum of solace—Douglas hadn't determined Bridget to be worthy of his staying in Cuyler Junction either.

❧

After three days on the road with Elmer before they parted ways, Levi slowed his horse to a trot as he neared the town. How many places had he traveled through since leaving home?

He'd lost count.

This town at least looked to have more to offer than the four or so previous ones he'd sauntered through on his route to wherever he was going.

A sign boasting the name *Cuyler Junction* greeted Levi, and several people walked up and down the boardwalk or drove wagons or rode horses on the main street. Levi spied a church, two saloons, a livery, a sheriff's office, mercantile, barber, post office, and stage depot in a business district surrounded by numerous homes at the edges.

His body ached from the long time in the saddle. Maybe he should stop for the night and bed down just outside of town.

Levi tethered his horse and entered Winrow's Mercantile. A woman with a round face and pleasant demeanor called from the front of the store. "May I help you, sir?"

"Do you have any fresh coffee?" Levi fingered the few coins he had in his pocket. While the shelves full of canned goods and the apple pie for sale on the counter beckoned him, Levi had to ignore the temptation. What little money he had left he must save until he reached his destination.

Wherever that might be.

"Right over there. Here, I'll show you." The woman led Levi to a pot of coffee. "Made it fresh just a bit ago. What else can I get for you?"

Levi thought of the lack of funds he possessed. It would be some time, if ever, that he would be able to buy things that weren't absolute necessities. "Nothing else, thank you."

"Are you just passing through?"

"Yes, ma'am."

She nodded. "If you need anything else, please let me know."

Levi pondered whether he should ask if there was any work to be had in the town. He figured if God wanted him to settle somewhere, that just might be how the Good Lord would orchestrate things. So far, there had been no work in the past four towns. Maybe this one was different.

"Ma'am, do you know if anyone is looking to hire a farmhand?"

The woman appeared thoughtful. "As a matter of fact, I heard they are looking for someone out at the Hammett place." She studied him. "Have you experience with running a farm?"

"Yes, I do."

"Please only inquire about the job if you are a forthright and honest man."

Levi swallowed. He might qualify for those two character traits, depending on whom one asked.

"They don't need any more problems, so if you're the type that's shady, unreliable, untrustworthy, and lazy, this position is not for you," the woman continued.

Levi raised his eyebrows. The woman must be a friend of the Hammetts to take this with such seriousness. "Don't plan on being shady, unreliable, untrustworthy, or lazy, ma'am. And I know farming like I know the back of my own hand."

"Then by all means, ride on out to the Hammett place and tell them Mrs. Winrow sent you."

He placed the coffee on the counter and dug into his pocket for some change. After paying, he extended his hand. "I'm Levi Callahan."

"Sue Winrow."

"Pleased to make your acquaintance."

Mrs. Winrow nodded. "Now from here, you travel two miles west. The Hammett farm is the second one on the right. You can't miss it because it has a large barn right before you get to the house."

"Thank you, ma'am." Levi tipped his hat and left the mercantile. Tomorrow he'd investigate the new job. But for tonight, he'd settle beneath the stars and pray that it was God's will he stayed in this town.

For Levi never wanted to make such a life-altering mistake again. One was enough to last him a lifetime.

The freshly plowed fields on the way to the Hammett farm caused Levi's heart to lurch. He missed working in the dirt. He missed the harvest and a cellarful of potatoes.

But it did no good living in the past.

He thought of Elmer and his recommendation to pray to God about everything, from the small things, to the big things, to the ones in between. This was a sizable request, but from what Elmer told him God's Word said, nothing was too big for the Lord. And if he'd truly surrendered to whatever God's will was for his life, then it made sense to seek that will.

Lord, if You are calling me here, please make it clear. I don't know what my future holds, only that I have given it to You.

Levi had always known *of* the Lord. But it took a life-changing event for Levi to come to *know* the Lord.

He spied the barn and beckoned his horse toward the Hammett home. The farm looked to be sizable, although rundown and in disrepair. He rode to the front of the house and noted a woman working in a nearby garden. Two small children, a girl and a boy, played in the yard.

Levi dismounted and met the woman at the garden. She stood, a shovel in her hand. "Good morning, ma'am." Levi removed his hat and held it in his hands. He offered up his best smile, although inside he wasn't so confident.

Of course, if the job was no longer available, Levi would move on to the next town knowing it wasn't God's will he stay here. Elmer mentioned that God always had a plan. Levi just had to be still enough to listen to that plan.

"Can I help you?" The woman didn't return his smile.

"Yes, I heard you were looking for a hired hand."

The woman's brown eyes widened before something akin to fear flashed across her face. "Who told you that?"

"Ma, who is that man?" A little girl of about three pointed her finger at Levi and peered around the woman's skirts.

The boy, his shoulders hunched forward, retreated to the dilapidated porch.

"Forgive me for not introducing myself. I'm Levi Callahan."

The woman ignored him and instead repeated herself. "Who told you we were looking for a hand?"

"A woman in town, Mrs. Winrow."

"From the mercantile?"

"Yes."

An older woman walked from the house then, wiping her hands on her apron. "Grandma, a man is here," announced the girl, once again pointing at Levi.

He couldn't help but smile at her round cheeks, flaming red hair, and inquisitive brown eyes.

"I'm sorry you rode all the way out here, but we are no longer looking for a hired hand."

The older woman gasped. "Norah?"

"You've already found a farmhand, then?" Levi asked. Disappointment welled inside of him.

"We just aren't hiring at this time." The woman named Norah began working again in the garden as if to dismiss him.

The older woman stood at the edge of the garden. "Norah, may I speak with you a moment?"

"Mama, I've already made my decision."

The older woman addressed Levi. "Please excuse us. We'll be right back. Norah, I must speak with you in private."

With a sigh, Norah followed the other woman inside the house. Levi could hear voices, but he couldn't make out the words.

"Did you ride your horse a long, long way?" the girl asked, standing next to Levi.

"Yes, I did." Levi tried to make eye contact with the boy as well, but he refused to look Levi's way.

"Did you ride from China?"

"China? No. Not that far." Levi chuckled at the girl's animated expression. "This is a nice place you have here."

"It's our farm. We live here with Ma and Grandma." The girl pointed at the boy. "He's my brother, but he don't speak much. 'Less he wants more food at the supper table."

Levi chuckled again. At least someone here seemed friendly. The girl's personality stood in sharp contrast to her ma's. "Is that so? Well, I remember when I was a young boy always wanting seconds too."

"You were a little boy?" The girl narrowed her eyes at him as if Levi told a bold untruth.

"Yes, a long time ago."

"Back when the Pilgrims came here?"

"Not that long ago."

"I'm Hazel, and I'm four, but I'm short for my age. Ma says I talk a lot."

Before Levi could acknowledge her words, Hazel spoke again.

"That there is Enoch. He's six, but he has less words in him than I do."

"Is that so?"

"Yes, Ma says he's shy." Hazel shrugged. "Not sure why anyone would want to be shy."

Levi grinned. "Reckon some folks are shyer than others."

"Are you shy, mister?"

"Can't say I'm as shy as Enoch over there, but I reckon I'm a bit shy."

The front door of the house opened and Norah and the other woman stepped outside. "Thank you for waiting," the older woman said. She took a step toward him. "I'm Bess Littleton. You can call me Bess. This is my daughter,

Norah Hammett. Norah, would it be acceptable to you for him to call you Norah?"

"Yes."

But Norah didn't sound too convincing.

Bess offered a smile. "I see you've already met my grandchildren, Enoch and Hazel."

Levi nodded. "Pleased to make your acquaintance, ma'am. Please call me Levi."

"Mama, I don't think this is a good idea," muttered Norah. Bess gave Norah a warning look that reminded Levi all too well of a few expressions his own ma had thrown at him a time or two when he was a young'un.'

"Mr. Callahan—Levi—do you have farming experience?"

"Yes, I do. Quite a bit of it in fact."

"And are you planning to stay until harvest if we offer you the position?"

"Yes, ma'am. I always aim to see a project through."

"We can offer you the job. Unfortunately, we won't be able to pay you until the harvest. However, you'll have room and board. Would this be acceptable to you?"

"Yes. I'm much obliged, ma'am."

Norah picked at something on her sleeve, and Bess pointed at a neglected white building about half the size of the bunkhouse back home. "You'll find accommodations in the bunkhouse just beyond the barn. Breakfast is served at sunup."

Norah folded her arms. "Are you an honest man, Mr. Callahan?"

A breath caught in Levi's gut. He was honest, even when no one believed him. His gaze met hers as she stared, awaiting his answer. "Levi, please. And yes, ma'am, I am honest. I keep my word."

"Good. I'll show you to the bunkhouse."

Levi followed Norah. "Is he gonna stay and work for us, Grandma?" he heard Hazel ask.

"I believe he is, Hazel."

"That's good because I want to ask him questions about the Pilgrims."

Levi chuckled to himself as he followed the sullen woman to the bunkhouse. It seemed that Hazel and Bess might be agreeable folks. Norah and Enoch might take some getting accustomed to. No matter. He wasn't planning to stay long. As Levi promised Bess a moment ago, he would assist with the harvest. After that, he'd determine his next plans, whether that meant staying in Cuyler Junction or moving on.

❦

Norah had to force herself not to stomp ahead of Mr. Callahan as she showed him his sleeping quarters. Had she not learned the first time with Ronald, the previous hired hand, whom she now realized her error in hiring?

Had she not learned from her husband and her father that men could not be trusted?

Had she been foolish not to heed the man's frightening words that day at the mercantile?

If so, then how had she allowed Mama to talk her into hiring another hired hand?

Yes, they needed one. Yes, she'd informed Mrs. Winrow of the necessity of someone to assist with the farm. Yes, things were dire. But now that someone actually arrived, Norah had second thoughts.

Especially after the episode in town where she'd been threatened about the advertisement. Of course, Norah hadn't told Mama about that. No sense in upsetting her.

Anxiety washed over her anew at the man's coarse confrontation at the mercantile, the note she'd found, and sighting him outside the church. What would he do when he discovered the new hired hand at the Hammett farm?

"Your daughter is quite the talkative sort," Mr. Callahan—Levi—said, interrupting Norah's thoughts.

"Hazel? Yes, she does enjoy prattling on."

"Enoch doesn't seem to be as talkative."

Making no response to his comment, Norah stepped up the one slanted stair onto the bunkhouse's porch. Levi rushed ahead of her and opened the door.

At least the man was courteous.

She turned to face Levi, nearly bumping into him as he gazed into the room. "This is where you'll sleep. It needs some repairs, but I think you'll find it suitable."

"It's fine, ma'am. Thank you."

"I must warn you that if I become aware of any dishonest dealings, I'll fire you without pay."

She watched a strange shadow flicker over the man's face before he answered. "No need to worry. I'm a hard worker and I'll help you turn your farm around in no time at all."

Turn her farm around? She fought the pride that welled within her. If Douglas hadn't left...

"Very well, then. I'll leave you to get settled. You can stable your horse in the barn. Breakfast is at six, supper is at five, and there is also a noonday meal."

"I look forward to some good cooking. Can't say as I've had that in a while."

Norah squinted at the man. She'd always been leery of drifters. Would the man be safe to have around her children? Mama would say to put it in the Lord's hands, so Norah would endeavor to do that. Perhaps she'd also ask Mama to pray about the situation.

"Would you like me to start on anything in particular? Reckon it won't take me long to get settled."

"We need to begin plowing the fields. Planting season is upon us. With the early thaw, we could have started earlier, but..."

Her words faltered. No sense in divulging their hardships to the man. He wouldn't be here long. "I'll be near the house preparing the garden area if you have any questions. The tools and the plow are here in the barn, the horses are in the corral."

"Thank you." His eyes met hers, and she quickly looked away and scurried out of the bunkhouse.

Hoeing the fertile earth once again in preparation for what she hoped to be a successful garden, Norah's thoughts invaded her mind. Why did she mention needing a hired hand to Mrs. Winrow? Perhaps the man who'd threatened her need not know she'd hired a hand. Of course, in a town as small as Cuyler Junction, news traveled fast.

The man's harsh words in the mercantile filled her mind. *"And don't you tell no one neither."* Perhaps she would ask Mrs. Winrow if she knew who the man was or maybe Norah should develop the courage to talk to Sheriff Perez about him.

The most perplexing question was why would someone care if she'd hired a hand to assist her with the farm?

Mama reminded her once again why they needed a hired hand when they'd met in the house just minutes after Levi accepted the position.

"Now, Norah, you know we'll never be able to plow the fields and bring in a harvest on our own. Are you willing to lose the place before you give up a bit of your stubbornness?"

Mama hadn't understood then, and she hadn't understood now. It wasn't just a matter of stubbornness. They wouldn't be in this position if Ronald hadn't stolen numerous tools they'd been forced to replace on account since they had no other way to pay for them.

No one had ever seen Ronald again, and their tools were never recovered.

What if Levi Callahan was the same way?

CHAPTER FOUR

THE FIRST SEVERAL DAYS went well, and on Saturday morning, Levi once again awoke to the sound of the rooster's crow. He stretched his arms overhead and peered out the dirty bunkhouse window. The farmland, the river just beyond the freshly tilled land, and the mountains in the distance stole his breath. He belonged on a farm. Tending to the earth. Planting seeds and watching nothing grow into something. Hard work invigorated him.

He slid his arms into his sleeves, buttoned his trousers, shaved, and headed toward the house. The aroma of bacon flooded the air, and he hastened his pace. For all the weight he'd lost during his week in jail, he'd for certain gained it back with Bess's and Norah's cooking.

Levi had immersed himself into preparing the land, fixing a few fences, and contemplating ideas for extensive repairs around the farm. Bess welcomed him, as did Hazel. Enoch spoke two words to him since he'd arrived, and Norah kept to herself. He observed the wariness in Norah's every glance.

It was the same wariness he experienced himself.

Levi stepped onto the sloped porch with two broken boards and entered the house. Dishes clanging, Hazel's chatter, and Bess's acknowledgment greeted him.

"Good morning, Levi. Did you sleep well?"

Not even Ma had ever cared if he'd slept well. "I did, thank you."

Bess smiled at him and nodded toward the table. "Have a seat. Breakfast is nearly done."

Levi was about to object and ask if there was anything he could do to help when Hazel perched next to him. She climbed on the chair, her legs dangling as she swung them. For the past couple of breakfasts, she'd asked him about the Pilgrims. Good thing he'd paid close attention to the subject in school all those years ago.

Hazel folded her hands beneath her chin and scrutinized him. "I want to know all about the Mayflower. Was it scary riding on the ocean in a big boat?"

Hazel was so enamored with that part of history, even though Levi reiterated he hadn't been a Pilgrim. "It took a long time on the ocean to reach what is now the United States. There was all kinds of weather—rain, wind, sunshine. Days upon days being aboard a ship with no land in sight." Levi recalled enthusiastically absorbing any book he could read during his school days. Since there were none at home besides Ma's rarely-touched Bible, he had efficiently finished his book learning so his teacher would allow him to read one of the many books on her shelf—her own personal collection including stories about America's founding, Christopher Columbus, George Washington, Abraham Lincoln, and the industrial revolution. Hazel reminded him much of himself in her zeal for learning.

"What did you eat when you were on the Mayflower?"

Levi attempted to recall what he'd read about the Pilgrims' diet while aboard the ship. "Salt pork, hard tack, and lots of fish."

"Did you have to eat oatmeal? I don't much like oatmeal." Hazel blanched, closed her eyes, stuck out her tongue, shivered, and pretended to gag. "Bleh."

Levi chuckled at her dramatic way of things, and glanced up to see Norah watching him.

He couldn't decipher her expression. Should he remind Hazel once again he wasn't alive during the time of the Mayflower? Tell her she should always eat oatmeal no matter how much she detested it? Say nothing?

When he again met Norah's gaze, she hastily set the plate on the table and returned for the pitcher of milk.

After breakfast, Levi stood, pushed his chair in, and took his plate to the sink. "Much obliged for the meal, Norah and Bess. It was delicious." He then focused on the young boy across the table from him. "Enoch?"

Enoch slowly raised his head. "Yes, sir?" he mumbled.

"Since it's Saturday and you don't have school today, I could sure use a good hand out in the fields today with rocks and such."

Enoch blinked rapidly, looked down at his half-eaten piece of bacon, and returned his attention to Levi. "Yes, sir."

"I'll head to the fields then." Levi retrieved his hat from the hook near the door.

"Before you go…" Bess peered up from handing a washed dish to Norah. "Would you care to join us for church tomorrow?"

"I'd like that, ma'am."

⸻ ❧ ⸻

Levi did not have any fond memories of Pa. Working alongside their fathers enabled many boys to grow with knowledge, work ethic, and a closer relationship with their fathers. Not in Levi's case. He'd never done anything right in Pa's eyes. As he grew older, Levi realized that to Pa, he was nothing more than a workhorse. His father took for granted Levi's strength, capability, hard-working inclination, tenacity, and stalwart determination.

While not Enoch's father, Levi hoped the time spent teaching the young boy about farmwork would be a heartening experience.

"I'd like to further expand the crop area, but with all this rock, it's near impossible."

Enoch stuck his hands in his trouser pockets and nodded, causing his worn hat to fall over his eyes.

"We'll hitch up the horses to the wagon, fill it up, and unload the rocks on the farthest southern area of the land. It's already mostly rock over there anyhow, and unusable. What do you think?"

Enoch peered up at him. "Reckon so."

"Of course, we won't be able to finish it all today, and this coming week we need to get the crop in, but if we could move some of it, I'd consider that an accomplishment."

"Can I help?"

"I need a hard worker to help me, and I think you'd be just the one."

Enoch stood up a bit straighter. "I can do my book learning faster so I can help with putting the crop in."

Levi's jaw went slack. It was the first time he'd heard the boy say more than a couple of words at a time. He cleared his throat and figured he ought to respond to Enoch what with the way the young'un gazed up at him with expectation. "I think I heard your grandma saying that your ma teaches you here at home, is that right?"

"Yes, sir."

"Book learning always comes first, so we wouldn't want to rush that too quickly." Levi rubbed his jaw. "But what if I do some other chores while you're doing your schooling and such, and then in the afternoon, we work together to get this field planted?"

Enoch's head bobbed. "Yes, sir. I'd like that."

A twinge of guilt overcame Levi at Enoch's enthusiasm. The young boy was eager to be accepted. If something happened here like it had back home and Levi made the mistake of protecting someone who didn't want protecting...if he had to leave again, it *would* devastate Enoch.

He would have to promise himself that nothing and no one would take him from the Hammett farm, from this family, or from the town of Cuyler Junction. He'd make that vow to himself, along with all the other vows he'd made. He'd do his best to ensure this little boy with his too-large hat, scuffed boots, and willingness to learn how to farm had an honorable mentor.

And Levi would be that mentor.

⁂

Norah filled the bucket with water, grabbed the ladle, and ventured toward the far end of the field where Levi wielded the plow on an untilled piece of earth. He'd accomplished much in his days on the farm, and with the ground thawing sooner than usual, the opportunity to plant crops and hopefully have a better harvest than last year looked promising.

Ma and Hazel had taken immediately to Levi. Norah reserved her opinions. Hadn't her last hired hand started off the helpful sort? Hadn't Douglas been a charming man when she'd first met him? Hadn't Pa pledged to love Ma all his days before he decided to up and leave?

The irony always struck her when she thought of how she'd vowed not to marry a man like Pa. When she was nine, he'd left and never looked back. Ma worked as a laundress in Boise City to support them. Every evening without fail, Ma would stand at the window of the humble room they rented at the boarding house and watch for Pa.

He never returned.

Instead, two days after Norah turned fourteen, Pa's body washed up on the banks of the Snake River. The sheriff speculated he'd been drunk when he ventured onto the frozen river, only to slip through into the icy water below. His body was found by some miners.

Pa had left her twice.

Ma mourned the loss of the man she'd loved, even though he hadn't returned that love. Until she'd rekindled her childhood friendship with Doc Farnsworth. Norah suspected her mother's fondness for the doctor went beyond mere friendship, but that she'd rejected Doc's overtures for marriage due to loyalty to Norah and the children.

While Norah promised herself never to marry a man like Pa, she'd done that very thing when, at eighteen, she'd married Douglas Hammett. A charming and adventurous sort with a wanderlust staying in one place could never satisfy, Douglas divorced her two years ago. He hadn't wanted any money from the rundown farm he'd taken a substantial banknote out on—he'd only wanted to rush to the Comstock Lode in Virginia City to try his hand at mining silver.

So, causing a scandal, he publicly divorced her, kissed her on the cheek, and rode away without once looking back.

Now much wiser, she determined that never again would she surrender her heart to any man. Nor would she trust a hired hand not to steal the tools that made earning a living from the land possible. Mr. Schreffler at the bank, in a moment of mercy, had loaned her the funds to purchase replacement tools, although now Norah wasn't sure she'd be able to pay off that additional loan in a reasonable amount of time.

As she drew near, Levi halted the horses, removed his hat, and wiped the sweat from his brow with his forearm.

Norah dreaded what she must say to him, and her stomach knotted. She much preferred avoiding any type of conflict.

Levi dipped the ladle into the bucket. "Much obliged for the water."

She waited until he'd satiated himself before planning her words. "Levi?"

"Yes?"

Norah shoved aside the realization that the man was downright handsome with his dark blond hair, hazel eyes, and broad shoulders.

Although, once upon a time, she'd deemed Douglas a handsome man as well.

She set the bucket on the ground and folded her arms. "I overheard you asking Enoch if he'd assist you in the fields today." She sighed, praying for her next words. "I would thank you kindly not to allow the children to become attached to you, especially Enoch."

"I'm not sure asking him to assist me hauling rock will encourage him to become attached to me."

Norah squinted into the sun, and he shifted so he stood at an angle to block it from shining in her eyes. "Hazel will recover from heartache, but Enoch…" Her precious little boy—the more sensitive and tender one of the two—had begged his father not to leave. He'd attached himself to his pa's leg and wailed as Douglas attempted to push him away. For several nights afterword, Enoch cried himself to sleep. Nothing consoled him. Not Norah, not his grandmother, not Hazel, not Doc Farnsworth, and not the reverend.

"When Enoch cares about someone—and then they leave—he holds all his pain in here." She patted her heart with her hand.

"I don't plan on leaving anytime soon, ma'am. As I promised Bess, I'll be here until harvest."

She wouldn't ask him his plans after harvest for that was none of her business. However, Enoch could easily become attached to Levi in that short amount of time. "And if you change your mind?"

"I won't."

His confident declaration gave her pause. How could he be so sure? If Payne succeeded in coaxing the land from her or if she couldn't pay her bills and afford to keep it; if the man at the mercantile took revenge on her for hiring Levi, or Levi decided on his own staying at the Hammett farm wasn't something he determined to do...

"You have to understand that I have to protect my children. A drifter wanders onto my property and seeks a job. You said you were an honest man, but I don't know if you've been in trouble with the law, been in jail, are a drunkard, or the like."

"Rest assured, I don't imbibe, and I'm a law-abiding man." Levi put the ladle in the bucket and stepped toward her.

"You have to understand my position on the matter. My former hired hand robbed us, and he too, promised to stay until harvest. My mother and I simply cannot afford another situation like the one he put us in due to his deceitfulness."

"Ma'am, I'm of no mind to cheat you in any way. Working hard for room and board and honest pay—even if I wait until after the harvest—is what I aim to do."

"Ronald assured us of much the same."

Levi kicked at a dirt clod. "And do you judge every man by the character of one?"

"It's hardly one man I'm judging your character by." Her annoyance flared. Levi knew nothing of what she had endured at the hands of Ronald *and* Douglas.

"I realize there is nothing I can do to convince you of my integrity, but I assure you I wouldn't have been as eager as I've been to start the tilling, plan for harrowing, and subsequently get the seed in the ground in a timely manner if my aim was less than honorable."

Hadn't Douglas charmed her much the same way with his zeal for becoming a farmer? His earnestness to carve a living from the land even though he'd only previously worked as a freight hauler before they married? Hadn't he purchased the farm with an assurance to her and to Mr. Shreffler of his steadfast commitment?

A commitment he had no intention of keeping?

"And if you change your mind about farming?"

"I won't."

"But if something else were to come along that garners your attention or demands you leave this farm before the harvest, what then?"

Levi squared his shoulders, but his voice remained calm. "Barring an unfortunate accident where I am unable to work, my plan is to remain here."

His eye connected with hers, and Norah desperately wanted to believe him. To believe he wasn't like those who'd deserted her before.

"Ma'am, I will do what I can to earn your trust, but you have to give me that chance."

He was right, of course, and Norah chastised herself for giving into arguing with the man. She released a deep breath thereby releasing some of the tension in her shoulders. "You are right. Please do forgive me. You deserve a chance, and you have done nothing to make me believe you'd fail at keeping your word."

"I do understand your concerns, especially with your son, and I will respect those concerns."

"Thank you."

"I know it's none of my business, but what happened to your husband? Did he pass?"

It would have been far easier if Douglas *had* passed. Levi was right, it was none of his business, but she might as well tell him. "I suppose you should know before you hear about it in town."

His gaze didn't leave her face.

"My husband, Douglas, divorced me." Even now, at the devastating rejection, tears misted her eyes. Pain for herself, but even more so for Enoch and Hazel, who would grow to adulthood without the father who helped bring them into this world. "Douglas always had a restlessness about him." She shrugged, willing herself to maintain her composure as the words popped from her mouth without stopping. "The farm bored him. The steady and consistent, every day the same as the next, became mundane, and when he heard about the Comstock Lode in Virginia City, Nevada, he left."

"I'm sorry. I had no idea."

"Of course not. How could you? But Douglas's choice did provide ample opportunity for gossip surrounding such a scandal. Some don't look kindly upon a divorced woman."

His brow furrowed and a faraway expression settled in his eyes. Was he, too, thinking as the townsfolk had? Would he now leave the farm? She should never have shared such details with a stranger. Norah bit her lip. At least if he did so, she had saved Enoch any further heartache.

Levi drew in a long breath. "Reckon people can be mighty hateful when they choose to be."

Not the words she was expecting him to say.

Norah peered behind her to see Enoch standing on the porch. She couldn't ascertain his expression from this distance, but he likely wondered if she'd finished speaking with Levi so he might join the farmhand in the duties Levi mentioned that morning.

She reverted her gaze back to Levi. Perhaps a change in subject was in order. "It might be forward of me to ask, but why do you not own your own farm? A man with such agricultural knowledge wouldn't be content working as a hired hand."

Something—sadness, perhaps—flashed in Levi's eyes. "I've only worked two farms, this one and with my pa on a piece of land he rented. Things didn't work out with Pa, so here I am. It is my dream to own my own farm someday, but until then, this suits me fine."

"Ma?"

Norah turned to see Enoch standing behind her.

"Can I please help Levi now? I've been trying to be patient."

It was the first time since Douglas left that he'd spoken more than a smattering of words here and there. Emotion welled in her throat at her son's expectant expression.

"Yes, you may."

A slight smile jotted across his lips. "Thank you, Ma."

"Are you ready to help me haul some rock?"

Enoch bobbed his head up and down. "Yes, sir, I am."

"Doesn't matter how much of it I haul away, there's always more." Levi plopped his hat on his head and offered her a reassuring nod. "We'll be in for supper."

Her heart jolted as she watched the two walk side by side toward the edge of the tilled land. It should have been that way for Enoch and his pa. Although only four when Douglas left, Enoch had idolized the man. The man who spent infinitesimal time with his son and even less with his daughter. He just couldn't be bothered. Douglas hadn't been a *bad* father, but he *was* an absent father. At the farm in body, but never concerned with the cares and thoughts of his family. Douglas's choices affected Enoch more than anyone, and the child suffered greatly because of it.

Lord, please heal my little boy's heart.

Levi's arms ached from the hard work of lifting heavy rock, carrying it to the wagon, and then unloading it again. But it was a good ache.

Enoch lugged a jagged lava rock, his thin arms straining beneath the weight, and hoisted it into the wagon. Levi patted him on the back. "You're doing a fine job, Enoch."

Oh, but to have heard those words even once from his father. To hear he was worth more to Pa than just a hand.

"Reckon my stomach is rumbling."

"Your ma will be happy to hear you're hungry."

Enoch's hat slid over his eyes, and he raised it on his head. "When can we plant?"

"Soon. There's much to be done to the earth before it's ready. Hauling rock among them." Levi paused. "I couldn't have accomplished this much without your help. Thank you."

"You're welcome. Say, do you think Ma is making cookies today? I heard her say something to Hazel about it this morning."

"Could be that she is. There's only one way to find out. Let's finish up here and see if there are some cookies waiting for us at home."

Home.

Yes, Levi could see this as his temporary home.

"Are we finished?" Enoch's hopeful expression drew Levi from his musings.

"Yes, we are. My stomach's rumbling for cookies."

Enoch giggled. "Mine too. 'Cept sometimes Hazel eats the dough all gone before it's baked."

<hr>

After their discussion earlier that day, Levi and Norah had come to some type of understanding. She'd been wounded in life just as he had by someone she loved.

True to Enoch's inkling about cookies, Norah and Hazel had baked some, and much to Enoch's relief, Hazel hadn't eaten all the dough.

A friend of the family and the town doctor by the name of Farnsworth, arrived for supper. Levi discovered he liked the man immediately and hoped to find a friend in him. Doc, as he preferred to be known, invited Levi to wander outside with him after supper.

"Are you finding you like Cuyler Junction?"

"I am. People seem friendly enough." Levi wouldn't share with Doc his experience was that people were friendly until they decided one wasn't worth their kindness.

Doc smoothed a hand over his bald head. "Reckon that's good to hear. I've lived here for about ten years, and I've seen folks come and go. Of those who remain, most are benevolent—Reverend and Mrs. Svenson, the Winrows, who own the mercantile, and, of course, Bess and Norah."

"I have yet to meet the Svensons, but look forward to doing so tomorrow at church."

Doc leaned against the corral post and peered into the distance. "Are you finding you like the work?"

Levi recalled Norah's initial hesitation in hiring him and their subsequent conversation earlier that day. If she knew he'd just been released from jail, she likely would have dallied longer at offering him the farmhand position—if she would have offered it to him at all.

"Yes. Reckon farming's all I've ever wanted to do."

"Own your own farm or hire on?"

"Wouldn't mind owning my own farm someday if the Lord wills it, but for now this suits me." A thought slipped into Levi's mind unannounced. Did Ma or Jay miss him at all?

"I would be remiss if I didn't mention that I care deeply about this family, so please don't give any of us any reason to doubt your intentions are anything but honorable."

Levi appreciated the man's loyalty. "I won't, sir."

"What with the hired hand that stole from Norah last year and some other personal things in her life, it's been tough."

The personal things Doc referenced likely pertained to her husband's choice to divorce her. "She mentioned the hired hand."

"Shame it all happened. Everyone in town seemed to like the fellow, and he never gave any indication of deceptiveness before he made the choice to steal. After that, Norah has a right to be leery of anyone who wanders onto the farm."

Did Doc doubt his integrity as well? Before he could ask, Doc continued. "Anything you can do to help the family won't only be appreciated by them, but by me as well."

"I aim to do my best."

"Much obliged for that. This family means a lot to me, especially Bess." A grin covered the older man's face. "I think I may have loved her from the moment I met her."

Levi had pondered whether there might be some affection between the two.

"We've known each other since our school days but were apart for many years. We've been courting for a while, and I've asked for her hand in marriage. So far she hasn't relented. But I'm a patient man. I just turned fifty, but I still have a lot of healthy years ahead of me." He stroked his graying beard. "Is there someone special for you back home?"

Levi hadn't thought of Criselda much since he'd left. "I was engaged, but she decided I wasn't the one for her."

"I'm sorry."

He wasn't sorry because it had given him a chance to determine who Criselda truly was *before* he made a lifetime commitment. "It was for the best. I'll be more cautious next time." If there was a next time. In actuality, matrimony might not be for him at all. Seeing how his parents shared a loveless marriage and if all women were like Criselda—deserting the man they professed to love when things went awry—remaining unmarried suited him. Criselda hadn't even the confidence in him to hear his side of what happened that day with Shipley.

Maybe women weren't worth the trouble.

As if to read his thoughts, Doc continued. "Not all women will be like the one who broke the engagement. If God wills it, you'll be a married man someday. If not, you'll go about your days as a bachelor."

"I've recently been learning about God's will and yielding my life to Him."

"It's a lifelong process."

Elmer mentioned something similar.

"It's getting late, so I best be on my way." Doc extended a hand. "I'll see you at church tomorrow."

Two hours later, as Levi rested his head on the hay-filled pillow on his bed in the bunkhouse, he offered a prayer to the Lord who'd guided him to the Hammett farm.

Because for the first time in his life, he'd found a place where he felt he belonged.

CHAPTER FIVE

THE CHURCH CAME INTO view, and Norah thanked the Lord once again that this was a place of acceptance, even for a woman divorced by her husband. Congregants totaled approximately thirty, and she'd found friends here, with the exception of Payne's mother and his sister, Bridget.

She surveyed the area just in case the man from the mercantile decided to lurk about again. Thankfully, Norah saw no sight of him. Perhaps the man had left town and she'd fretted needlessly about the entire situation.

Levi assisted her, Mama, and the children from the wagon. Hazel jumped up and down as if she hadn't just been lethargic an hour earlier when awakened. "Can we go play before church starts?"

"Yes, but you only have a few minutes, and please stay close by."

"I will." Hazel wrapped her arms around Norah's waist. "Love you, Ma!"

Without awaiting a response, her vivacious daughter bounded toward her best friend, Bethany, one of Mrs. Winrow's granddaughters.

Enoch, on the other hand, expressed a lackluster eagerness to partake in games before church. He stood, shoulders drawn into his ears and eyes wide.

Mama immediately went to visit with Doc, leaving Norah, Enoch, and Levi standing near the wagon.

It was then Norah noticed much of the milk from Enoch's cup at breakfast was crusted on his face. Norah kneeled to his height, licked her finger, and swiped at the dry milk framing Enoch's mouth.

He wigged and writhed, fidgeted, and squirmed. "Ma," he whined.

"I'm almost finished. Please hold still, Enoch."

He wrinkled his nose the second time she licked her finger and removed more milk from his chin that had formed the beginnings of a milk beard.

Levi chuckled, his laughter contagious, and Norah attempted to stifle her own amusement. "It's not so bad is it, Enoch? I just want to ensure you're presentable for church."

Her son scowled.

Levi stood next to her, a grin still lighting his face. "With that expression, you would have thought you were asking him to do his least favorite chore."

Norah straightened and released a giggle, noting it felt good to laugh. "Indeed. For all of Hazel's theatrics, I daresay Enoch has a few of his own."

Levi's gaze connected with hers, and she felt the warmth of a blush.

A tap-tap on her arm caused her to avert her eyes to the source. "Yes?"

"Ma, can I please go inside now?"

"Yes, you may. She smoothed a wayward tuft of hair before Enoch slithered to the church.

Perhaps they would have a successful crop this year so she could purchase fabric to sew him a new shirt to replace his faded Sunday best. His trousers, falling above the ankles on his gangly legs, needed replacing as well. She sighed. Enoch's narrow shoulders slumped as he neared the stairs leading into God's house. "He's so painfully shy." she muttered, not intending to voice her inner musings. Hazel ran and laughed with her friends, her red braids bobbing behind her. "While Hazel is so lively."

"Reckon God made us all different. I was shy like Enoch as a boy."

Levi's statement reminded her he still stood nearby. "You were?"

Her gaze met his again, and she witnessed a tenderness in the depths of his hazel eyes. "I was. I'm sure it's difficult not to fret, what with being his ma and all, and Enoch has been through a lot, but he'll be all right."

"I—thank you."

Hazel and Bethany bounded toward them. The two stood peering up at Levi. "This is our hired hand, Levi. He was on the Mayflower," said Hazel.

Bethany's eyes rounded and her mouth formed an "o". She gasped. "I never knew anyone who was on the Mayflower 'afore."

Hazel shrugged. "Me neither until Levi came to our house one day."

"Were you scared riding on the Mayflower?" Bethany asked.

"I wasn't on the Mayflower, but I have read a lot about it." Levi's words did little to halt the girls' captivated attention, and Norah stifled a laugh. As if Hazel's constant intrigue wasn't enough, now Bethany joined in.

Hazel tapped on Levi's arm. "Weren't you scared of the sharks in the water?"

"There were sharks, whales, and other fish, but the Pilgrims were safe aboard the boat."

Bethany bobbed her head. "I'm glad you were safe, Mr. Levi. That musta been daunting."

"Come on, Bethany, let's go play some more before church." Hazel clasped her best friend's hand and together they swung their arms as they skipped away.

"I'm sorry, Levi," said Norah. "We read about the Mayflower last month, and ever since then she's been fixated on the story."

Levi laughed. "Reckon it makes me famous to have been a Pilgrim on the Mayflower. At least in Hazel's and Bethany's minds."

From the corner of her eye, Norah watched as Payne approached them. He wore a tailored suit far too elaborate for the likes of Cuyler Junction. When he reached them, he cast a glance at Levi, then lifted her hand and placed a kiss on it. "Good morning, Norah."

"Payne."

He regarded her for a moment before releasing her hand and focusing his attention on Levi. "I don't believe we have met. I'm Payne Deaton."

"Levi Callahan."

The men shook hands. The differences between their appearances was profound. Levi stood several inches taller with broader shoulders than Payne. His hair was a darker blond, while

Payne's was a whitish blond. Levi's trousers and plaid shirt, likely his Sunday best, paled in comparison to Payne's frock coat and matching gray pinstriped trousers. Levi's scuffed brown boots showed much wear, unlike Payne's low laced, shiny black shoes.

"Mr. Callahan, what brings you to Cuyler Junction?"

"I'm the new hired hand at Mrs. Hammett's farm."

Norah sucked in a breath. Would Payne share with others that she had hired someone? Her thoughts reverted to the horrible man in the mercantile a few weeks ago, the same one she'd seen outside the church last Sunday. Surely Payne wouldn't associate with the likes of such a person.

"The new hired hand?" A shadow crossed Payne's face as a muscle in his jaw twitched. "May I have a word with you, Norah?"

"Please excuse us," she said and followed Payne a few steps away from Levi. Payne leaned toward her and lowered his voice. "You know how fond of you I am."

A fondness Norah most certainly did not reciprocate.

When she said nothing, he continued. "As such, you also must understand I do worry about you." Payne nodded toward Levi. "The man is an outsider. We know nothing about him. Perhaps you ought to reconsider hiring him."

"I've already hired him, and just because one is an outsider doesn't make them a bad person any more than being a Cuyler Junction resident makes one an upstanding citizen."

Bridget Deaton sashayed by with Mrs. Deaton, and bile rose in Norah's throat. Gossip about Bridget's dalliance with Douglas was confirmed when Norah came upon them kissing in the grove of trees on the farm.

The pain struck her like no other pain had, not even the ache of her father leaving or receiving the news of his death.

Norah blinked several times, willing the memory to fade.

Bridget paused, allowed her perusal of Norah to travel from the top of Norah's head to her worn shoes. She pursed her lips, acting as though she'd eaten something distasteful, then looked down her too-narrow nose at Norah.

Payne placed a hand on her arm, extracting Norah's attention from Bridget's scrutiny. "All I am saying is that I hope you'll use caution. We know nothing about this man."

"Thank you for your concern."

"Of course."

Norah edged her way back toward Levi, who was chatting with the mill owner, Mr. Holloway. Payne followed her, mumbling something beneath his breath she couldn't decipher.

"Norah!" Orlene Svensen rushed toward her and captured Norah's hands in her own. "I was hoping to speak with you." Her brow creased. "Despite my best intentions, I forgot to retrieve the trousers Audney has for Enoch yesterday when Geir and I were paying her a visit."

Norah adored the reverend's wife, a dear woman who at times lapsed into her native Norwegian tongue.

"The trousers?"

"Yes. Audney's youngest has outgrown them, and Audney thought perhaps Enoch could use them."

"Thank you. I would appreciate that as Enoch has been growing like a weed." Norah thought of Enoch's too-short trousers. "Do you think I ought to wait until Bard's health improves before I pay her a visit?"

Orlene shook her head so rapidly the perfectly-round gray bun atop her head wobbled. "No. I mentioned you could perhaps be by Wednesday or Thursday afternoon. I know Audney would appreciate the visit, especially since she hasn't been able to leave the house much with her husband so ill."

"Thursday afternoon would be an opportune time. Might I take her some raspberry preserves?"

"She would expect nothing in payment, but she does find your preserves from those plentiful raspberry bushes on your property quite delicious."

Norah marveled at how the Lord would once again provide. "I will plan a visit. Thank you, Orlene."

Orlene gave her a hug. "You're more than welcome."

Something in Payne's eyes flickered, and he stared at Norah a moment before acknowledging Levi once again. "Might I speak with you in private?" Levi agreed and followed Payne to the maple tree on the edge of the church's property.

Norah greeted the reverend standing at the church's entrance, then took a seat in the fourth pew on the right-hand side next to Hazel. Enoch sat between Hazel and Mama, and Mama sat chatting with Doc.

Mama leaned forward in the pew and gently touched Norah's arm. "Doc has asked me to accompany him for a drive after church." A glint touched Mama's eyes. "I should be back before supper. Will you and the children be all right?"

The hopefulness in Mama's countenance provoked mixed emotions in Norah. She knew Doc's company made

Mama happy and that she had grown fonder of him in recent months. The man was kind and thoughtful and clearly doted on her mother. But would he someday be an honorable husband?

"Yes, we will be fine. Have a pleasant drive."

"Oh, we shall." Mama's broad smile overshadowed Norah's concerns, and Mama returned her attention to the man who'd clearly won her heart.

◆◆◆

Levi crossed his arms and surveyed the man demanding his time. He wasn't blind. Others may miss the hints of discomfort radiating from Norah when interacting with Payne, but Levi didn't. If something unnerved Norah about this arrogant man, then it would be best to keep an eye on him.

"You needed to speak with me?"

"Norah is beautiful, isn't she?" Payne's gaze never veered from Norah until she had disappeared into the church.

Levi stared after Norah. "Yes, she is." He'd thought that the first time he'd met her, but even more so this morning, when she'd emerged from the house in her Sunday finest wearing a faded pink calico skirt and a pale blue shirtwaist. She'd fashioned her wheat-colored hair into a bun, and one strand had escaped during their drive to church, framing her lovely face. Her light brown eyes lit whenever she spoke of her children, and he'd noticed the dimple in her left cheek when she smiled. Yes, Norah Hammett was a beautiful woman.

Payne tugged on his jacket lapels. "I'm fond of her and hope to someday ask her to court me." He rocked back and forth on his heels and grinned, although the smile never reached his eyes.

"Is that so?"

"It is."

"Who Norah decides to court is not my business." Although Levi doubted she'd choose someone like Payne. He'd seen how she flinched when the man kissed her hand.

"Unfortunately, she is a divorced woman."

"Through no fault of her own."

Payne shrugged. "Be that as it may, my interest in her has caused some consternation, especially on the part of my sister, Bridget." His eyes narrowed. "Of course, Bridget has no fondness for Norah."

Levi had seen the way Bridget, a woman who resembled her brother so strongly they could be twins, regarded Norah only minutes ago. Clearly Payne overestimated the care Levi would give about the opinion of a pompous peahen.

"Is there a reason you wanted to tell me this?"

Payne's expression flickered. "I merely wished to impart some friendly advice about getting too comfortable here in Cuyler Junction. Once I marry Norah and take over the farm, your assistance will no longer be needed. You'd be wise to begin contemplating your travel plans. I don't foresee Norah retaining the Hammett surname for long."

If Payne wished to impress with his fancy vocabulary, he failed. Sorely. And if this poppycock-spouting man with an oversized opinion of himself thought he could scare Levi away, he'd be disappointed.

Levi met Payne's eye. "I will only leave when Norah tells me herself she no longer needs my help." He then made his way to the church, leaving Payne to fume and bluster.

CHAPTER SIX

OVER THE NEXT COUPLE of days, life hummed along. Norah finished planting the garden, churning butter, and preparing lessons for Enoch.

She shielded her eyes from the sun and observed the freshly harrowed rows, all ready for planting, and joy bubbled within her. For the first time, she felt hopeful they would be able to not only bring in a decent crop, but pay a bit extra on the banknote and the tool loan. For the first time, she'd be able to dedicate more attention to the children's schooling, her garden, and canning because she didn't have to spend as much time in the fields.

And for the first time since Douglas left, Enoch was the little boy he'd been before his father made the decision to walk out of their lives.

Levi came into view, and she filled the bucket to take him some water. He whistled the strains of, "What a Friend We Have in Jesus" while tending the soil. He hadn't heard her approach, and she took in the sight before her.

His tan shirt, spread across the expanse of his broad shoulders, detailed his muscular back. His hair, curling slightly at the ends, peeked from beneath his hat. Levi wasn't only a dapper man, he was also a godly, kind, and generous, as well as a dedicated employee.

Levi pivoted to face her then, and she hastily averted her gaze as her cheeks grew warm.

"Hello, Norah."

His deep voice, one she'd so recently become accustomed to, prompted her to once again focus on him. Norah momentarily forgot why she came to the field. "I—hello." She grappled for the words. "I—well—I thought you might be thirsty."

"Thank you." He ladled some water from the bucket. "Mighty fine day today. Blue sky, sunshine, a slight breeze, the smell of soil, and..." he paused as if he may well say more. The warmth of his smile sounded in his voice.

When had she become nervous around him? Must be the fact she had much on her mind, for it couldn't be possible she might have begun to grow fond of the man whom she'd hired.

Or could it?

She shook her head and mused about the absurd notion. Norah reminded herself once again that she'd never again trust a man, especially with her heart.

"Norah?" Levi's brow furrowed.

"I'm sorry. I must be somewhat discombobulated." What of the easy camaraderie they usually shared? "Have you noticed the weather today?" *Of course he noticed the weather. He'd just mentioned it.* "I best return to the house and check on the children. Enoch was working on some arithmetic problems."

"He's a smart boy."

Pride welled within her. "Thank you. And thank you for allowing him to assist you."

"You're welcome."

"And for being patient with Hazel and her belief that you were a Pilgrim on the Mayflower. She's only four, but thinks she's much older, hence the reason she also has book learning lessons every day."

His hazel eyes met hers. "Your children are blessed to have you as their ma."

Something akin to pain registered in his gaze.

"You don't speak much of your mother. Are you two close?"

Levi's lips twitched downward. "Not at all. She isn't like you are or like Bess is. I'm not sure my ma ever experienced joy."

She rested a hand on his arm. "I'm sorry."

"We can't choose what family we're born into, but I fully believe we can choose not to be like them. My pa is a difficult man. Filled with discontent and a critical spirit. If there's one thing I aim to be if I'm ever a pa someday, it's to be the opposite of him."

"Given what I've seen of you in the short weeks you've been here, you're nothing like your parents."

A comfortable silence between them ensued, and Norah thanked the Lord for the friend she'd found in Levi Callahan.

On Thursday after the noonday meal, Norah packed the two jars of raspberry preserves and a loaf of bread in a burlap sack and rode to Audney's house. The spring air invigorated her, and she inhaled deeply as the breeze tickled her face. Nothing compared to Idaho in the spring.

When she and Mama moved to Cuyler Junction, Audney was one of the first women Norah met. The gracious woman in her forties, a younger version of her mother, Orlene, reminded Norah that not everyone gossiped about another's misfortune. Rather than contribute to the wagging tongues in town, Audney came alongside Norah and prayed for her.

Norah tethered the horse and walked toward the humble cabin. Thankfully, Audney had two nearly-grown sons who assisted with the farm's upkeep since her husband, Bard, hadn't been well for several months.

"Oh, do come in!" Audney ushered Norah inside. The sickly scent of illness permeated the air, and Norah offered a prayer heavenward for both Bard's healing and for Audney as she cared for him.

Norah handed Audney the preserves and bread, and tears filled the older woman's eyes. "You know how I enjoy your raspberry preserves. Thank you."

"How is Bard?"

"Doing as well as can be expected. We keep praying. Doc has given us some tonics to assist with the pain, but…" Audney sighed. "We're not giving up yet. He's resting right now, which eases my mind since he's been so tired as of late. Come, I have something for Enoch."

Audney led her around the corner to the table and handed her two pairs of trousers. "Bard, Jr. has outgrown them, and since he's only a few years older than Enoch, I figured they'd fit him quite well."

It was Norah's turn to hug her friend. "Thank you. I can't tell you how much this means to me. I was just praying the crop would enable us to purchase fabric so I could sew Enoch a new pair. He's been growing so much lately."

"That's what friends do—bless each other. Now tell me, how are things on the farm? How is Bess? The children?"

"Mama is doing well. Of course, she is fond of Doc, and he's fond of her. I think the only reason she hasn't agreed to marry him is because she fears leaving us." Norah smoothed her hand over the trousers. "Hazel is doing well and is as spirited as ever. Enoch has started talking a bit more, thanks to Levi Callahan, a man we hired to assist us on the farm." At the mention of his name, the heat climbed up Norah's neck. Would her trusted friend notice?

Audney tilted her head toward Norah. "I hope he won't be a cad like that last hired hand."

"So far he has proven to be just the opposite. He works hard, and Enoch has taken a liking to him."

"And is Enoch the only one who's taken a liking to him?"

The heat radiated from her neck to her face. "Mama, who, of course, cottons to nearly everyone, likes him, as does Hazel."

"What does Norah Hammett think of this new hired hand?"

"He's so opposite of Douglas in nearly every way, not that I'm comparing them, mind you—all right, I am, and yes, were it not for the fact that I've promised never to trust a man with my heart again, I might be growing fond of him."

Audney laughed, and they continued chatting about Audney's three sons, recipes, and sewing patterns. Norah refrained from telling Audney about the man in the mercantile. It would only cause her to fret, and the dear woman did not need that in addition to the stress she endured with Bard's ill health.

After a pleasant two hours with her dearest friend, Norah bid Audney goodbye, stuffed the trousers into the saddle bag, mounted her horse, and headed home. A scan of the sky above indicated rain clouds. They needed the moisture for the crops so she'd not complain; however, the pleasant spring weather had been most welcome.

Thoughts of Levi entered her mind. While she struggled with trusting him, she did have to admit he'd been an answer to prayer. With his hard work, they may have a decent or even prosperous harvest. That paled in comparison to the changes she'd seen in Enoch due to a man who spent time with her son as a pa should.

As Douglas should have.

And Audney was right in her assumption of Norah's growing feelings for him.

A burlap sack on the side of the road with something wiggling inside of it caught Norah's attention as she rounded the bend. She slowed her horse, and as she drew nearer, she heard a yipping noise.

A dog, perhaps?

Norah dismounted and approached the bag. She pulled it open to reveal a tan-and-gray puppy. "Oh, you sweet little animal. Who would leave you here all by yourself?" She snuggled it closer and patted its fluffy fur. Wouldn't Enoch and Hazel love a new pet? The pup began licking her face, and she set it carefully on the ground.

Just then, someone seized her upper arm and spun her around with such force she nearly tripped over her feet. Norah righted herself and looked up into a familiar face.

That of a man with an unruly beard and dark, evil eyes. His fingernails dug into her upper arm, and she winced and attempted to remove herself from his grasp. In response, he dug his fingers deeper into her flesh. "Hold still!"

Norah kicked him hard in the shin. In response, he jerked back and muttered a stream of curses that burned Norah's ears. She endeavored to extract herself from his clutches by pulling backwards and continuing to kick him.

He was much too strong for her and gripped both of her arms in his fleshy hands, nearly lifting her off her feet as he simultaneously pulled her toward him. He bent his head toward hers and sneered between gritted teeth, "What did I tell you about hirin' someone on yer farm?"

"I—please—you're hurting me."

"I done asked you a question, and I'm wantin' an answer."

"I don't understand why I can't hire someone to work on my own farm." Her voice trembled as she spoke, and her heart pounded in her ears. There were no houses in this stretch of area. Only acres upon acres of farmland. Would one of Audney's sons hear her if she screamed?

Likely not, but she did it anyway.

Norah's high-pitched shriek reverberated through the otherwise quiet woods. His hand clamped over her mouth, pressing hard against her teeth. "Shut up!"

Her heart beat violently in her chest and she fought for breath.

"Please release me." Norah's words emerged muffled due to the man's hand still pressed firmly against her mouth.

Worry snaked through her.

Finally, after what seemed much longer than a few seconds, he removed his hand. "Do not scream again." The man's close proximity unnerved her, and she turned her head to escape the foul odor of his breath. He reached one hand up toward her face, and for a moment she feared he would strike her. Instead, he wrenched her chin back into his vision, causing a searing pain from her right ear down to her shoulder. "I told you not to hire no one, and you done it anyway."

"I just need to be able to bring in a good harvest. To pay the banknote." Suddenly, things like banknotes seemed trivial in light of what the man could do to her.

And no one would even know.

How long would it be before Mama determined she wasn't returning home? Mama knew Norah and Audney could talk for hours. Would she assume they were still conversing even after a lengthy amount of time?

Would seeking the man's mercy persuade him to release her? Promising to fire Levi? Apologizing? Or doing the exact opposite and acting as though his harsh treatment of her didn't matter? As if she could feign bravery.

Lord, please, please help me.

Several seconds ticked by, fear paralyzing her as the man pressed closer to her, his grip even fiercer.

"Sell the land."

"I..."

"Do you want to ever see your young'uns again?"

"Please unhand me." Norah's voice again quivered as the panic rose within her.

"Seems to me you got a little girl about yea high." He removed one hand and held it at waist height. "Purdy little thing with red hair. And there's a boy too. Scrawny fella of about six or so. Ain't there some other woman who lives with you too? 'Bout forty somethin' with reddish hair and a nice smile?"

He *had* been watching her and her precious family. At least often enough to provide physical descriptions. Norah shuddered and struggled to remain calm.

The man squeezed her jaw between his fleshy fingers and thumb. "This will be your last warnin'. Fire the hired hand and sell your land. You got one week. And don't you tell no one about our meetin' like this." Spittle flew from his mouth, landing on Norah's cheek, and she retched. "If you tell anyone, them kids of yours might up and disappear. Or that ma of yours. Or you."

She could not—would not—allow anything to happen to her family.

"One week? Please can you make it two? I need time to pack up our belongings and to fix..." she paused and contemplated her next words. "To fix the broken wagon. It's not fit to travel any distance beyond to town and back. Please. That will give me time to send a telegram or a letter to my relatives back East and have them send for us. I'll need the wagon to take us to the nearest train depot so we don't have to take the stage." Ramblings were all they were, really. There was nothing wrong with the wagon and she had no relatives back East who would send for them.

He shook his head. "One week."

A thought unfolded in her mind. "If you wait two weeks, the farm will be worth more to whoever buys it because the wheat will be fully planted and some of the crop will have already started to grow. The new owner will have less to do to make the farm productive."

The man's eyes narrowed, and the muscle beneath his right one twitched. Sweat shimmered on his face, collecting in the pores of his bulbous nose.

Norah shivered. What if he didn't release her? Harmed her further? She should have brought the rifle hanging above the fireplace. But the thought of needing it just to visit Audney hadn't occurred to her.

"You do make a point about the wheat and all." His eyes bored into her as if he could see she'd been fetching for excuses. "You fer sure gonna leave in two weeks?"

She stifled her relief. "Yes. And I know of a couple of people who wish to buy the farm. But I need a little more time."

He squeezed both arms again and twisted her left one behind her back. She cried out in pain as the tears slid from her eyes.

"You better not be lyin' to me, woman."

"I'm not. Just unhand me and allow me to go on my way."

"Be a sad shame if something happened to you right here." He leered at her and brushed her cheek with a grimy finger. "Yep, would be a sad shame. Ain't no one would be the wiser." He nodded toward the nearby river with its icy spring water tumbling over the rocks. "Also be a sad shame if you somehow drowned. 'Course, then you wouldn't own the land no more." He released a mirthless chortle, the deafening and maniacal tone echoing through the trees.

The man shoved her then, and she toppled backwards and fell hard on the ground, barely missing the puppy, who'd planted herself in the dirt near a downed log.

The man approached her, his loud footsteps thudding, and yanked her off the ground and onto her feet once again. "I will be watchin' you, and I will be waitin' to be sure you keep yer word. You got yerself two weeks to sell the land and leave Cuyler Junction. If not..." the unsaid words knotted her stomach.

He reached down and scooped up the puppy, and shoved it back into the sack.

"Please. Can I take her home with me?"

"Don't need it anyhow." The man thrust the sack toward her, nearly causing Norah to lose her balance once again. "Now git. And don't tell no one about this. Not the sheriff, not your ma, and not that hired hand." He waved a slightly bent forefinger inches from her face.

"I won't."

"See that you don't."

He spun and lumbered toward his horse.

Norah collapsed to her knees, shaking violently. Tears streamed down her face as she thanked the Lord for His Providence. She alternately rubbed each arm, noting that he'd clawed her so hard that he'd likely caused bruising and welts.

She needed to get home.

Or go back to Audney's.

Which was closer?

Norah scrutinized the area around her. Confusion reigned, and for a moment, she forgot where she was and how she'd come to be here.

Clarification soon returned.

Home was closer than returning to Audney's. But what would she tell Mama, who would know immediately something had happened?

She couldn't tell her mother anything—or at least she couldn't tell her anything about the man who'd attacked her.

Never once in all of her twenty-six years had she ever lied to Mama. Not once in her twenty-six years had she been less than forthright. But Mama and the children's lives depended on her obeying the man's orders.

The puppy yipped, and she nuzzled against it, allowing its warm fur against her chin to calm her.

She slowly trudged to the horse and, with great effort, mounted and beckoned the animal toward home. Her head ached from being flung to the ground. Her arms throbbed. Could she tell Mama she'd been thrown from her horse?

That she'd not seen a fence or a tree and had nearly run into it?

How would she explain to Mama they must leave their home? And where would they go once she sold the farm? She'd spent time late into the night calculating numbers, and the meager amount they'd receive after paying the banknote—if someone paid her the amount the farm was worth—would do nothing to secure a future for them. She, Mama, and the children wouldn't even be able to start over with a place to live.

Yes, they could return to Boise City after days of travel, and Mama could again hire on as a laundress. Norah could gain employment by mending or cleaning. But they would have nothing.

She thought of Payne's offer to buy the farm. Of Mr. Schreffler, the banker telling her someone in the next town was interested in her farm. Of Mr. Medina, the sour-faced friend of Payne's who'd also offered to buy her land.

Why was it everyone wanted to buy her land? Why couldn't they leave her well enough alone?

If Douglas decided she was worthy of staying faithful and remaining married to, would this ruthless man be forcing him to sell?

And why did Payne, Mr. Medina, and the banker's friend want a dilapidated farm with a rundown barn and a house that shifted and allowed plentiful cold air through the cracks of its poorly constructed walls during the brisk winter?

It made no sense.

Unfortunately, she was unlikely to find neither answers nor a reasonable resolution any time soon.

Norah hugged the puppy close and wearily rode down the road she'd taken so many times before. She lifted her prayers of gratitude for the Lord's protection over her along with a petition that He would safeguard her family in the days to come.

CHAPTER SEVEN

ONCE ON HER PROPERTY, Norah dismounted and washed up in the creek on the edge of the land not far from the road leading to the corral. Kneeling, she splashed her face with water, re-braided her hair, and dusted off her mud-caked skirt. She grasped the reins and led the horse the remainder of the distance to the corral while holding the puppy close. Enoch and Hazel would be thrilled about a new pet.

"Norah?"

Levi's voice interrupted her thoughts.

"Norah? Are you all right?"

Tears blinded her vision. She couldn't tell Levi what had happened. While she didn't know him well, she knew him well enough to figure his reaction to such an occurrence wouldn't be one of indifference.

"Hello, Levi. I had an accident on the way back from Audney's."

Enoch's trousers. She needed to remember to remove those from the saddlebag.

Peculiar how such an unimportant matter entered her mind at that moment.

"An accident?"

"Yes," she squeaked, keeping her focus on the road ahead. The less he saw of her face and her disheveled appearance, the better, for he'd never believe her story otherwise.

"Norah, please, can you stop walking for a minute?"

She did as he requested and focused her attention on the puppy. "I found this little one on the road between Audney's and here."

"Norah?" Levi lifted her chin gently with his finger, and she saw the concern in his eyes. "Are you all right?"

"I will be."

She barely knew this man who so unexpectedly arrived in their lives, yet the longing to fall into his arms and seek comfort against his broad chest was overwhelming. To be protected, safe from the threat she'd just experienced.

"You had an accident?"

Norah hastened a breath through her parched throat and willed the remaining lump of fear to subside. "I—yes. But I'm all right." She again peered into his eyes, eyes that had become familiar to her in the passing days. Doubt lingered in his expression. While being thrown from her horse would certainly cause tumult, it likely wouldn't cause the emotional tempest she currently experienced.

Should she tell Levi the truth?

Lord, I beseech Thee for wisdom.

A perusal of the area assured her Mama and the children were likely in the house doing schoolwork or preparing supper. "You can't tell a soul," she whispered.

"About your accident?"

"Yes."

"I promise."

Trust had never come easy for her. If Levi *did* tell the sheriff, the man would be arrested, but what if there were others involved in this scheme to remove her from her land? Her children's and Mama's lives would still be in danger.

"I need your word, Levi."

"You have my word. But if it was just an accident..."

Tears flooded Norah's eyes, and she was helpless to stop them. "They want the land."

"Who?"

"I don't know his name. He..."

Levi stiffened. "Did someone hurt you?"

She shrugged, noting that the motion caused discomfort in her aching arms. "I don't know who he is. He made me promise to fire you, sell the land, and move or else..." The sobs came quickly then, and she covered her mouth with her free hand lest Mama or the children hear her.

As if to read her mind, Levi gently led Norah by the elbow to the barn. "I want you to tell me everything." He released her briefly to tether the horse.

The words spilled out in between more sobs, and Levi listened intently until she finished. She told him she'd previously had a confrontation with the man at the mercantile before Levi arrived in Cuyler Junction. She shared about the note and how she thought she'd seen him outside of the church that day. She then described her attacker in detail. "Have you ever seen a man who fits that description in town?"

Levi's brow wrinkled. "I haven't seen someone like that, but I've not been to town much."

"I promised to acquiesce to the man's demands." She trembled at the memories of the man's hands on her, his leering gaze, his threats, and how he knew so much about Enoch, Hazel, and Mama. The angst of knowing he'd been watching them. Norah shared it all with Levi. How her assailant clutched her arms, shoved her, held his hand over her mouth after she screamed. How she'd kicked him and attempted to escape. About the puppy in the bag and how she rescued it. About the names of the three men who wanted to purchase her land. And finally, the horror of something happening to her family because she'd shared the details.

Levi clenched his fists at his sides, and a vein throbbed in his jaw. "We need to tell the sheriff. This man can't avoid punishment for what he did to you."

"But if he finds out, he'll take revenge and harm my family." She choked on another sob. How could she make Levi understand that, while she agreed the law needed to know of this man's actions, doing so would jeopardize her family?

She and Levi discussed it at length before he agreed not to ride into town and tell Sheriff Perez. "But you have to promise me you won't go anywhere by yourself."

"I promise. And, Levi, please don't tell Mama."

"I won't tell your ma. Also, I'd like to at least ask around town and see if I can find out who this man is." He took her hand in his. "I will find whoever did this to you."

⁕

Rage swept through him. Someone had hurt an innocent woman once again, and the desire to protect her and see that justice was served was immense.

He didn't know Norah well enough to draw her into his arms and comfort her, although the urge was strong. Standing in front of him in obvious pain with her shoulders slumped, hair in disarray, and her dress muddied, she reminded him of a helpless bird that had fallen from its nest and needed to be returned to safety.

Levi gently wiped a tear trailing down her cheek. "Did he hurt you in any other way?"

Please, Lord, let the answer be no.

"He did not."

Levi exhaled a sharp sigh of relief at the answered prayer. *Thank You, Lord.*

Memories of Mrs. Shipley's face registered in his mind. The woman who rarely emerged from the Shipley residence, had been outside that day Levi was assisting Shipley, also the mayor of the town, with mending the fence. Shipley had arrived home smelling of whiskey. Supper wasn't on the table, and his wife bore the brunt of his anger. Witnessing his fist connecting with her face was something Levi would never forget.

In an instant, Levi was running across the field with heart racing and anger coursing through his veins. With strength even he didn't know he had, Levi pulled the much larger, much heavier Shipley away from his wife.

Shipley muttered a string of oaths before throwing the first punch in Levi's direction, connecting with his jaw. Levi returned a blow, all the while instructing Mrs. Shipley to get into the buggy and seek safety at a friend's house.

Mrs. Shipley limped to the house, and Levi again advised her to remove herself from her husband's presence lest he once more lose his temper with her.

But the woman instead apologized to her husband, her voice quivering as she blamed herself for not having supper ready and promised she'd never be so neglectful again if he'd only give her another chance.

Levi hadn't known which occurrence bewildered him more—watching Shipley lay a hand on a woman or that woman groveling at his feet even after suffering abuse.

Years of farmwork built enough muscle on Levi's frame that winning the altercation against Shipley came easily.

But the man promised Levi would spend time in the jail for what he'd done. He assured Levi everyone in town would know what kind of man he was to attack not only his own employer, but also such a prominent town citizen.

Levi had stepped back as Shipley staggered to his feet. His terse words still rang in Levi's ears. *"You'll be sorry you ever intervened."* He then raised his voice several octaves and bellowed for Mrs. Shipley to make him supper.

The sheriff arrested Levi the following day, and Levi suggested the lawman speak with Mrs. Shipley about the incident. But instead of acknowledging what her husband had done, the woman mentioned she'd fallen down the stairs of their extravagant home.

Levi suspected that wasn't the first time Shipley abused his wife, nor would it be the last unless he was stopped. The difference between what really happened and a carefully plotted lie caused Levi to spend time in jail, and lose everything that mattered to him.

He inhaled a sharp breath. At least Mrs. Shipley eventually came forward and left her husband. Shipley could no longer harm her. And while Levi promised he'd never get involved again with another matter that didn't pertain to him, he now knew he couldn't keep that promise.

The protectiveness that rose within him that day with Mrs. Shipley paled to what he now felt.

He would do what it took to protect the Hammett family.

Some of the burden had lifted from Norah's shoulders after telling Levi about what happened. They had two weeks to determine what to do. Surely an answer would soon be revealed.

Norah retrieved Enoch's trousers and Levi tended to the horse while Norah carried the puppy into the house. Hopefully the dog would distract her family enough from Norah's troubled countenance and disheveled appearance.

Mama was reading the Bible as part of their school lesson when she entered. "Norah? What happened?"

"I had a small accident, but I'm fine."

Mama gasped and held a hand to her mouth. "Are you sure you're all right?"

If she stood here much longer, Mama would see right through her veiled attempt to hide what *really* happened. "I did manage to find this puppy while returning from Audney's."

Hazel squealed and jumped up and down. Enoch's eyes rounded and he took a step toward Norah with outstretched arms. "Ma, can we keep her?"

She handed the pup to her son, and he immediately cuddled it.

"Can I hold him, Enoch?" Hazel sidled up alongside her brother.

Enoch nodded, but he didn't relinquish their new pet.

Hazel beamed as the puppy licked her hand. "I'm gonna name her Mayflower."

That evening after putting Enoch and Hazel to bed, Norah and Mama sat in the two rocking chairs. Norah hoped to finish hemming the trousers Audney had given to Enoch, while Mama worked on a quilt. To Mama's credit, she didn't inquire further about Norah's "accident", although tightness lingered in Norah's chest from the guilt of not being forthright.

Mama reached for another square of fabric. "That Levi sure is a kind fellow. I don't know what we would have done without his help."

"Yes, he is."

"He's handsome too."

Norah inclined her head toward Mama. "He is kind and he is handsome, but I have no inclination of ever falling in love again."

Even though she said the words, Norah knew they weren't true. She'd already lost her heart to Levi.

"Who said anything about falling in love?" A hint of a smile crossed Mama's face.

"Once upon a time, I believed Douglas to be kind and handsome. And, once upon a time, you assumed the same of Pa."

"That is true." Mama continued to rock in her chair, her countenance thoughtful.

"And what of Doc? He's proposed, hasn't he? You should accept his offer of marriage." Perhaps if Mama agreed to marry him, she wouldn't have to worry about a place to live should Norah be forced to sell the farm. Mama would have a home, and Norah and the children could reside somewhere in Cuyler Junction with Norah working for room and board. She could take in mending or maybe Mrs. Winrow would hire her at the mercantile. "I want you to be happy, Mama."

"I am happy."

"You could accept Doc's marriage proposal."

"I could. At this time, you and the children are my top priority. When I'm reassured that all is well here and you're able to handle the farm—whether that's because Levi remains here as a hired hand or whatever the case may be—then I'll consider Doc's offer."

"Mama…"

Her mother held up a finger to stop Norah's objections. "Then and only then will I consider Doc's offer. He understands fully the situation we've found ourselves in."

Relief flooded through Norah. While she first and foremost wanted Mama to be happy, and Doc proved himself a worthy beau for her, Norah did need Mama's help. "Thank you. You know how much I appreciate you."

"Well, it always has been just us, with a brief juncture including Douglas."

"And through all of that, you remained loyal to me." Her throat thickened with emotion.

Mama wrapped an arm around her, and Norah rested her head on Mama's shoulder. "Thank you."

"And thank you, Norah. A mother couldn't ask for a more godly and devoted daughter."

Norah basked in the warmth of her mother's love. The Lord had blessed her with a mama who was faithful, caring, and steadfast.

CHAPTER EIGHT

LEVI CARRIED HIS DISHES to the dry sink. He hadn't slept well last night mulling over what he should do about Norah's attacker. He would have to keep his promise to her, but he didn't want to risk her being harmed again. There were times he wasn't near the house due to the Hammett farm's expansiveness. Would her assailant leave her alone until the two weeks lapsed?

Hazel prattled on, telling Mayflower all of her plans for the day before dashing outside with Bess and the pup to see if any flowers had sprouted from the seeds she and Norah planted last week. Enoch remained at the table stirring his food around on his plate.

"Is something wrong, Enoch?"

"Can I help you instead of doing my book learning?"

Norah wiped her hands on her apron and approached her son. "You can help Levi *after* your book learning is completed."

"Aw, Ma. That ain't fair."

Norah planted her hands on her hips. "That isn't fair."

"You don't think so either?"

Levi watched the interaction between the two as a hint of a smile pulled at the corners of Norah's mouth and her eyes danced with amusement in response to Enoch's statement.

During his growing-up years, Levi's own mother rarely smiled. He recalled once, when Jay won the spelling bee at school, that for the briefest of moments a grin replaced Ma's typical dour expression.

Yet here at the Hammett household, smiles were given freely. Even when little boys complained about schoolwork.

"Enoch Douglas Hammett, are you being cheeky?"

He thumbed a finger at his chest. "Me? No, Ma, not me. Not Enoch Douglas Hammett." Guilt flashed across his face, and he alternated between staring at his food and peering up at his mother from the corner of his eye, all the while attempting to hide his own silly grin.

Norah took a seat at the table. When she raised her arm to place it around Enoch's shoulders, Levi saw the pain etched in her face due to the injuries. He inwardly winced. If he could protect her from everything that might ever happen, he'd gladly do it.

"I know you like to assist Levi in the fields," Norah was saying, "and I'm grateful for a son who is a hard worker."

"And a farmer. Don't forget that, Ma. I'm a farmer now."

"Yes, and a farmer. However, you must finish your schoolwork first."

The boy released an exaggerated sigh. "Yes, Ma."

"All right. Finish your breakfast, see to it that your chores are finished, and I'll meet you back here for your arithmetic lesson after I tend to the washing."

Enoch shoved an enormous bite of egg into his mouth.

Levi returned his attention to Norah. "How are you today?"

She would know the meaning behind his words.

"Bruised and sore, but so grateful I was able to..."

Enoch was peering up from them, questions in his gaze. Levi again focused his attention on the boy. "I'm thankful you'll be completing your book learning in a timely manner, Enoch, as I'm in need of a helper to go to town with me on an errand."

Enoch's head bobbed up, and he chewed faster. Taking a full swallow, he pushed his chair from the table. "Can I be your helper, Levi? I can get my writing and arithmetic done the fastest I've ever done it."

Levi's eye caught Norah's, and she provided a slight nod. "All right, then. I'll plan to go right after the noonday meal."

"I'd like to stay and talk, but I've got chores to do and then arithmetic." Enoch flew out of his chair and was out the door before Levi could respond.

Norah retrieved a basket of items, including a primer and a slate, and set them on the table. "I've noticed such a difference in him. I owe that to you, Levi. Thank you."

"You're welcome." Levi didn't add that he would have given up all the farmland in the entire world just to have a pa who cared enough to spend time with him. Or a ma like Norah who cared about and loved her son. He dug two shiny pennies from his pocket. "I do have these leftover from my travel here. Would you be amenable to me buying Enoch and Hazel some candy at the mercantile?"

"If you're sure you want to spend it on that."

"I'm sure."

"You're going to spoil those two."

Levi tilted his head and lifted his shoulders. "Could be." He paused and changed the topic. "Do you need anything while I'm in town?"

Norah's eyes gleamed. "Thank you for asking. Yes, I do need some more flour since you're going to the mercantile. Please ask Mrs. Winrow to put it on account."

Levi plopped his hat on his head. "Will do. I'm going to ask around about the man who attacked you and give the description you provided."

"But you promised not to mention about what happened to the sheriff."

"And I won't, but I may ask him if he knows who the man is." He debated telling her his other plans or to leave it as a surprise.

He chose the latter.

"It will take us some time in town, but maybe later this week, I'd like to show you my plans for planting potatoes in the far corner."

Her mouth rounded into an "O".

Levi reminded himself this was not *his* farm. "If you're agreeable to potatoes."

"I just—Douglas was told this land wasn't conducive to growing that crop."

"Some of it's not. But there is a sizable corner section with the proper sandy soil where an old creek bed once was. I'd like to give it a try."

"If you think it would be advantageous."

"It's worth a try. Norah, you have extremely fertile soil here, some of the best I've seen."

They were interrupted by Enoch dashing through the door. He put his hands on his thighs and attempted to catch his breath. "Chores are done, Ma. I'm ready for my book learning."

Levi finished planting the remainder of the wheat. Already the first seeds had begun to sprout. He sauntered back to the house and once again surveyed the broken porch before joining the others for the noonday meal.

For the first time since Norah brought the puppy home, neither Hazel nor Enoch were holding it. Instead, Mayflower rested in a basket on a blanket near the fireplace.

Throughout the entire time of eating, Hazel shifted in her seat, bumping into her glass of milk and nearly spilling it. "Ma, can I please be excused?"

"You've only eaten a couple of bites."

"I know, but I'm just so static."

Levi joined Norah and Bess in laughing at Hazel's mispronunciation of the word "ecstatic".

"What are you static about?" Enoch asked, shoveling another bite into his mouth.

Hazel jiggled her legs and tossed her mother a pleading look. "Please, Ma? I have to show Levi my schoolwork. Then I'll eat again. Please?"

"All right, and then I want you to resume eating."

"Thank you, Ma!" Hazel bolted from her chair and ran into one of the two small rooms. She emerged seconds later, slate in hand. Sidling up next to Levi, she peered at him, eyes bright. "Can I show you something, Levi?"

Levi pushed his plate aside. "What is it, Hazel?"

"It's what I did today for school. Yes, I'm only four, but Ma teaches me just the same as she teaches Enoch."

Enoch grunted. "Except that you can't do arithmetic, reading, or writing yet."

Hazel's brows knitted together, and she pressed her mouth into a firm line. "Yes, I can, Enoch Douglas Hammett. I can do 'rithmetic, reading, writing, Bible, and history." She positioned the slate directly in Levi's line of vision. "I drew this just for you today. It's a picture of the Mayflower. Is that how it looked?"

Levi stroked his chin as he examined the drawing. Hazel tapped her slate pencil on the table beside him. "I wasn't a passenger on the Mayflower, but this does appear to be an accurate rendition of what I've seen in books, and I read a lot of books as a young'un. Every one I could get my hands on."

"It does?" Hazel squealed and clapped her hands. "See, Ma, I told you Levi would 'member what the Mayflower looked like even though it was so very long ago when he was a pass-ger. Do you see how I put the flag on the pole? And I even drew some designs on it." The little girl's words came in a wild rush. "That's not all!" Hazel slanted the slate vertically. "See those letters? Those are the letters 'H', and 'A', the first two letters in my name." She took a step back and beamed. "See, Enoch, I can do writing just like you." Her gaze fixated on Levi, awaiting his response.

"Those are nice letters, Hazel. The Mayflower picture is well-done."

A smile occupying her entire face shone as enthusiasm radiated from her. "Thank you." She traced the outer frame of the wooden slate. "I best go put it away for now and get to eating."

"Yes, that would be best since that's what you promised your ma."

Without a second more of dilly-dallying, Hazel reclaimed the slate and bounded toward her room once again.

Levi glanced up just in time to see Norah watching him. She mouthed the words "thank you", and he nodded in response.

Something about this family drew him. Drew him in to wanting to stay and farm for longer than the harvest.

But to do that, he'd have to break the vows he'd made to himself.

CHAPTER NINE

LEVI BECKONED THE HORSES toward town. If all went as planned, he'd return home with enough lumber to entirely redo the porch.

Home.

When had he begun thinking of the Hammett farm as *home*? He recalled breakfast when Norah thanked him for assisting with Enoch. Her gratitude and her pretty smile did something to him he couldn't quite explain. Of Enoch's excitement of working with him these past days after he'd finished his book learning and his inquisitive questions about crops, rocks, and a host of random things. Of Hazel's artistic rendering of the Mayflower and her misshapen "H" and "A" letters on the slate. She'd been so proud of her ability to write the first letters of her name. Of her naming the puppy after her favorite ship. Of Bess's ability to make him feel like part of the family.

He'd grown to care about the Hammetts in such a short amount of time.

Norah's face flashed again in his mind. She'd expressed thankfulness to him on more than one occasion for taking care of the farm duties, and especially for his assistance with Enoch. No one had ever expressed gratitude to him for anything. Certainly not Pa. Not even when Levi worked day and night hoping to secure his father's approval. All to no avail.

He thought of Norah again. Hadn't Levi vowed not to get involved with protecting someone after what happened with Mrs. Shipley? Hadn't he pledged not to care for another woman after Criselda's disloyalty?

Norah had changed that for him.

"Are we going to the mercantile?" Enoch asked.

"We'll go to the lumber company first. I'm hoping to trade some work for boards so I can fix your ma's porch."

Enoch sat up straighter, as if he was fourteen instead of six. "I can help you."

"Be much obliged for that."

The boy smiled as though Levi offered him the new toy train set at the mercantile.

Minutes later, Mr. Holloway pointed to the freight wagon. "Unload those boards and place them over here, stacked against the outside wall of the building."

"What about me, sir?" Enoch puffed out his chest. "I'm Levi's helper. Got a job for me?"

Holloway quirked a bushy gray-brown eyebrow. "Just so happens I do. Some nails spilled earlier today. If you could pick those up and do some sweeping for me..."

Before the owner could finish speaking, Enoch was agreeing to the task.

"Sir, a word before I begin," said Levi.

Holloway, a jolly-seeming sort with an ample girth and plentiful facial hair that compensated for the lack of it on his balding head, motioned for Levi to join him away from Enoch and the few customers moseying about.

"What can I do for you?"

Levi described Norah's attacker's appearance. "Have you seen a man around these parts that fits that description?"

Holloway scratched his head. "I haven't. But that doesn't mean he's not been in Cuyler Junction. Usually I spend all of my time here, at church, or at home. If he's not at any of those three places, it's likely I ain't seen him. Why do you ask?"

"I've just been attempting to locate him is all."

The mill owner seemed satisfied with his answer, and Levi lifted the heavy wood and did as Holloway requested. When he finished, he loaded the boards Holloway gave him as payment, and he and Enoch started down the boardwalk toward the mercantile.

"You did a fine job at the lumber company. Seems to me we might have to see about some penny candy at the mercantile."

"Really? And for Hazel too?"

"Yes, for Hazel too."

Enoch skipped alongside Levi. What would it have been like for Pa to have taken Levi to the mercantile for candy? Not because candy was important, because it wasn't. But because it would have created a fond memory, rather than the dismal ones of Levi's childhood he carried around with him.

They arrived at the sheriff's office. "Let's stop here for just a minute."

Enoch's eyes rounded. "I've never been in there before."

Levi took a deep breath. Entering the sheriff's office would bring back memories best buried of a week spent in a confined and acrid cell and treated as though an outlaw. He gripped the door and gathered his wits before he and Enoch stepped foot inside.

Sheriff Perez hastily removed his feet from the desk. Payne sat across from him, both of them puffing on cigars. The fetid odor clouded the air.

The sheriff stood and strode toward Levi and Enoch. "May I help you?"

Payne removed the cigar, leaned back in his chair, and glowered at Levi.

Levi preferred to discuss this matter at another time when Payne wasn't present, and in hindsight, not in front of Enoch. So instead, he devised another plan. "Hello, Sheriff. Thought I'd stop by and introduce myself. I'm Levi Callahan, the new hired hand at the Hammett farm."

Payne harrumphed. "You stopped by to introduce yourself to the law? Why when you won't be residing in Cuyler Junction for any sort of duration?"

Levi ignored him and extended his hand to the sheriff.

"Nice to meet you. I've been away for the past couple of weeks spending some time in other parts of the county. Crime has been next to none as of late here in Cuyler Junction, not that I'm complaining."

"Things are always like that here. Rarely is there any crime to speak of." Payne took another puff on his cigar, causing a ring of putrid smoke to rise into the air."

Sheriff Perez's expression remained stoic. "Are you a church-going man, Levi?"

"Yes, I am."

"Good to hear. And who might this young fellow be?"

The boy hid behind Levi, but extended his hand. "Enoch," he said, his voice muffled.

"Enoch. Well, nice to meet you both. Let me know if there's anything I can ever do for you."

"Thank you, sir."

Levi and Enoch then headed back down the boardwalk to the mercantile. Levi barely opened the door when Enoch yanked on his hand and tugged him in the direction of the counter. "Come on, Levi. Let's get me and Hazel some candy!"

Mrs. Winrow fetched a stool for Enoch, and he stepped up onto it and peered into the glass bowl full of candy. "My stomach is growling something fierce just thinking about those peppermint sticks."

Levi figured this was as fitting a time as any to ask the Winrows about the man. He once again offered the description Norah shared with him.

"I believe I may know of whom you speak," said Mrs. Winrow. "He has shopped here a time or two, mainly purchasing tobacco and canned goods. He always pays, so we don't have an account for him and don't know his name."

Mr. Winrow plunked a heavy crate on the floor. "I don't recall his name either, if he ever even mentioned it. He's a sour fella, that much I do know."

"Much obliged. If you see him, can you let me know?"

Mr. and Mrs. Winrow both agreed. Levi turned and perused the shelves of canned goods, baking items, prunes and dried apples, fabric, sewing notions, boots for both men and women, rope, axe handles, bullets, gun powder, and a stack of books. For a town Cuyler Junction's size, the mercantile housed nearly everything a person could want.

"Hello."

He stole his attention from the axe handles to the woman standing beside him. She fluttered her lashes at him, and while he recognized the traits of a flirtatious woman, he'd never be impressed when those lashes belonged to none other than Bridget Deaton.

"I saw you at church," she said, opening her eyes so wide Levi thought they'd pop out of her head. She added an exaggerated smile revealing perfectly-straight teeth. "I'm Bridget, Payne Deaton's sister."

"Levi Callahan."

She continued to gape as she wrapped a wayward tendril around her finger. "Are you in Cuyler Junction for long?"

"As long as I need to be."

She giggled, emitting an annoying, high-pitched grating noise dripping with insincerity. "I saw you earlier at the mill. Are you working for Mr. Holloway?"

"No, ma'am. I'm the new hired hand at the Hammett farm. Surely you've heard of it? About two miles west of town?"

A scowl replaced her counterfeit smile, and she stiffened her shoulders. "Oh, yes, I've heard of it. I should have known when I saw you sitting by Norah Hammett." At Norah's name, Bridget wrinkled her nose in disdain. "She's such a contemptuous woman. I merely hoped you were only sitting by her because the rest of the pews were full."

"No, I was sitting by her because I wanted to."

She held a hand to her heart. "I'm utterly flabbergasted as to why you'd want to sit by her at all, let alone work for her. You do know she is a divorced woman."

"Due to no wrongdoing on her part."

Bridget flashed a smile full of needles at him. "Believe what you wish, Mr. Callahan. Good day."

Mr. Winrow, who'd been standing nearby unloading crates, tossed a knowing glance Levi's way as Bridget stormed from the mercantile.

"Best not to become involved with anyone in that family, although don't let on that I told you so. The Deatons own this town."

Just like Shipley.

And Levi doubted there was much difference between Payne Deaton and the man who abused his wife.

<hr/>

Doc arrived for supper that evening, and Levi shared a camaraderie with the older gentleman with the witty sense of humor. After everyone finished their meals, Levi asked to speak with the doctor outside.

"What's on your mind, Levi?"

"A couple of things." He first asked Doc about Norah's attacker, learning Doc had never seen him before. "What do you think of Payne Deaton?"

Doc shoved his hands in his trouser pockets. "Can't say as I much care for the man or his family. Not that I want to speak ill of anyone, but there's just something about him. I know he's fond of Norah, but thankfully, I don't believe the feelings are mutual."

Levi doubted she shared Deaton's affection. The man reminded him of a dishonest, slithery snake. "I had the displeasure of meeting his sister in the mercantile."

"That family has caused the Hammetts a lot of pain."

Levi didn't want to gossip, but he *did* want to discern the opinions of a man who'd called Cuyler Junction home a lot longer than he had. "What about Sheriff Perez?"

"He's an honorable man."

Levi thought of Perez and how he'd been smoking cigars in the sheriff's office with the likes of Payne Deaton. "Is he friends with Deaton?"

"Not that I'm aware of. Perez hasn't been here long, but he garnered an excellent reputation up north as a sheriff. I was one of the first ones to meet him when he applied for the open position here in Cuyler Junction. Why all the questions about Perez and Deaton?"

Levi would keep Norah's confidences, but Doc's estimation of both men proved to aid Levi in the next steps he'd suggest Norah take to protect her family and keep her farm.

Norah and Mama finished their inside chores, and Mama had gone for a buggy ride with Doc. Norah was about to start the children on their studies when she noticed Levi unloading boards from the back of the wagon.

Enoch joined her at the window. "Ma, can I go help Levi?"

"Book learning comes first."

Enoch crossed his arms over his chest. "Aw, Ma…"

"What are those boards for?"

Her son's scowl relaxed into a smile. "He's fixing the porch, and he needs a good helper."

"Fixing the porch?"

Hazel wandered over, Mayflower a permanent resident in her arms. "Can I see?"

Norah shifted to the side of the window so Hazel could glimpse the ongoings as well, and Enoch tugged on Norah's arm. "If I hurry and do my book learning, can I go help?"

"Yes, you may."

She'd never seen her son move so fast as when he scampered to the table and started his bookwork.

Levi waved at her from near the wagon. How had he managed to purchase enough pieces to repair the cracked and damaged porch? She stepped through the front door and met him as he unloaded another board.

"Figured we needed to mend the porch before someone hurt themselves." The corded muscles in his forearms drew her attention.

"How were you able to secure the wood?"

"Traded Holloway for some work. Enoch helped me."

That Levi would take the time out of his day of a multitude of chores further endeared him to her. "Thank you."

Her breath hitched when he offered her a handsome smile.

Levi propped a board against the house and lowered his voice. "Mrs. Winrow may know who the man was who harmed you."

"You told her?"

"No, I just asked her, Mr. Winrow, Holloway, and Doc if they knew a man who fit the description. Mrs. Winrow mentioned it may have been a man who retrieved a few items at the mercantile from time to time, but always paid rather than putting the purchases on an account. She doesn't know his name. Norah, I think we should talk to Perez about it. Doc seems to think he is of sound character."

Recollections of that horrific day loomed in her mind and filled her dreams at night. She shook her head. "We have some time left to decide what to do. I've been praying about it, and thankfully, so far I haven't seen the man."

Levi rubbed the back of his neck. "I don't like it, Norah."

"I won't go anywhere by myself."

"You know he'll be back if you don't fulfill his demands." He reached for her hand and clasped his fingers around her palm, causing a flutter in her stomach. "Promise me we'll go to Perez in a day or two. I don't want anything to happen to you, the children, or your ma."

Tears misted her eyes at his concern. He was right, and from what she'd already experienced, it was unlikely her attacker would relent. Levi squeezed her hand. "All right," she whispered.

"Good. Reckon I best get to work if I'm to make some progress on our new porch before sunset."

Our new porch.

She liked the sound of that.

CHAPTER TEN

ENOCH AND HAZEL, MAYFLOWER in her arms, climbed into Doc's buggy with Mama and Doc for a picnic. Norah appreciated the time alone. The stillness in the air without Hazel's continual chatter and Enoch's pleading with her to be able to go the fields *before* he finished his schoolwork proved refreshing.

After mentioning something about an area of land he wanted to investigate for planting more potatoes next year, Levi saddled his horse and veered in the southern direction of the Hammett farm.

Next year. Was he planning to stay longer than the harvest?

Her heart thrummed at the thought.

Norah scanned the closest fields. Plentiful miniature green sprouts dotted the landscape for the first time in a year. Had Levi misspoken or did he truly intend to stay?

But what if she lost the farm?

The expectation for Norah to sell the land, move from the property, and yield to the man's demands remained troubling. While neither she nor Mama traveled to town alone, would the man find another way to achieve his goal?

Norah shivered despite the sun's warmth. For too long she'd struggled with trust of any kind. She tilted her head toward heaven, noting the brilliant blue sky directly overhead, and a few gray clouds in the distance warning of the potential for an afternoon thunderstorm. *Lord, please forgive me as I have failed to trust You as well. Yes, I put my faith in You all those years ago and surrendered my very life to You, but yet I don't have the belief that You can deliver us from this circumstance. An enormous obstacle for us, yes, but infinitesimal for Someone who knit my babies together in my womb and created the mountains, sunshine, and stars. Someone who sent His Son for the sins of mankind. Father, I am sorry. May Your will, whatever that be, be done in this circumstance. I only ask for Your protection and safekeeping over those I love.*

The tears dampened her cheeks, and she swiped them away. No matter what happened, even if her family must move to another home, the Lord would provide.

That same Lord caused a mere seed to bud and grow in the formerly-barren fields. Yes, such a mighty Creator would also deliver them from this current difficulty.

Her heartbeat steadied and calm replaced the anxiety.

She returned to the task of hanging laundry on the clothesline when she heard the sound of dirt crunching beneath wheels. An efficient perusal indicated Payne's buggy nearing the barn.

What could the man want?

Not long after Douglas left, Payne revealed his interest in her. An interest that was far from mutual. He reminded her of a chameleon—genial and willing to assist others at places like church—and self-seeking and miserly everywhere else. While she hadn't been as overt about it as she could have been, Norah suspected her rejection of Payne greatly frustrated him.

Payne exited the buggy and waved at her. "Hello, Norah." He brushed the sleeves of his topcoat and strutted in her direction.

"What brings you to the Hammett farm?" Norah dried her damp hands on her skirt just in time for him to take her right hand in his and plant a kiss on it.

"My dear, how are you today?" He pinned her with a roving gaze before his eyes tightened at the corners.

"I'm well."

"Good, good. Always good to hear." Payne rubbed his thumb over her hand before releasing it. "I come with an inquiry."

She clasped her hands before her, lest he attempt to make any further overtures. "An inquiry?" Norah scrutinized the man standing in front of her, with his white-blond hair parted perfectly down the middle, his slightly darker sideburns exactly the same length as they traveled the sides of his face, and the prominent groove below his nose that led to his mouth.

"Yes, an inquiry and a proposition all at once." He held his chin at a proud tilt. "As you may have realized some time ago, I am enamored with your beauty."

Something akin to disgust rose within her. "My beauty?"

"Yes, and of course your charitable disposition. As such, I have considered on more than one occasion asking if I might court you."

While the question was not completely unexpected, it did take Norah by surprise. After all, Payne's own sister had carried on a dalliance with Douglas.

"Do say yes. Should we later marry, which is my intent, you will live a life you've always dreamed of, which includes an elaborate house with a maid and a cook. Your children—if you wish—could be sent to a boarding school where they would receive the finest of education, all at my expense. You would have lovely dresses rather than..."

He motioned to her worn attire, and for the first time, Norah felt ashamed at her lack of fashionable clothing. Still attempting to recover from Payne's brash and presumptuous query, she was about to respond when he continued.

"You'll not have a want in the world. What do you say?"

Before she had the wherewithal to stop the words, they flowed from her mouth. "If I reside in your family's home, what of Bridget? What of your mother? Neither would enthusiastically embrace the thought of my children, my mother, and me moving into the Deaton household."

"Your mother as well?" Payne's eyes bugged before he lifted his shoulder in a half shrug. "Not a concern in the least. The house is large enough to accommodate four more people, and if not, we can easily add additional rooms." He averted his attention toward the road.

Waiting for someone, perhaps?

But whom?

"Payne, while I appreciate your interest, I will have to decline."

The downward *v* of his brow and the irritation that flickered across his countenance told Norah he was not amenable to her answer. "Is that your final decision?"

"It is. As much as I value your friendship, that is all I feel for you." *If that.*

His tone rose an octave. "It is your final decision and you don't plan to alter it?"

"I'm sorry, Payne, I..."

Something akin to fire blazed across his pale cheeks. "In that instance, you leave me no choice."

Fear splintered her heart and worry snaked through her. What could he mean that she gave him no choice? Her imagination could wander in a variety of directions, but Norah didn't have to wait long for him to expound.

"In that case, you leave me no choice but to purchase your land from you."

"Purchase my land? I've already told you I'm not of the mind to sell."

Another buggy rounded the corner, one she didn't recognize, followed by a man on horseback.

The hairs on the back of Norah's neck stood on end. Something wasn't right.

Mr. Schreffler, the banker, stepped from his buggy with papers in his hand, and the man who attacked Norah nearly two weeks ago dismounted from his horse.

And for a moment, she was barely able to breathe.

The man, exerting his oversized presence, sneered. "Do you need our help?"

"Good of you to arrive, Marcellus. Yes, I believe so." Payne nearly bowed as he took a step back and beckoned the wicked man.

Marcellus clenched his teeth. "I thought I done told you to sell the farm, woman."

Her chest tightened with fear. What if Mama and the children returned and Norah had inadvertently put them in danger? Would Levi return soon? He said once he plotted the area for potatoes, he'd retrieve her and show her his plans.

Father, please help me.

Payne extended his hand and pressed it on Marcellus's chest. "Allow me." In a rapid movement, he snatched Norah's wrist and clamped his fingers tightly around it.

She winced as he squeezed harder. "Payne, you're hurting me."

Payne stroked her cheek with his free hand. "If only you would have accepted my gracious offer for courtship and matrimony, then none of this would be necessary." A sinister smile touched his lips. "Mr. Schreffler, bring me the papers for her to sign."

Mr. Shreffler cowered near the clothesline. "I must disagree with this method of obtaining a signature. It would hardly do to have Mrs. Hammett sign it while under duress."

With two lengthy strides, Marcellus approached Mr. Shreffler and bunched the lapels of the man's jacket in his fist. "Give me the papers."

Mr. Schreffler, a fourth of Marcellus in size, shrank back. "I must dissent."

"You dissent and you'll regret it," said Payne in a sing-song voice. He again tightened his grasp on Norah's wrist.

"Payne, you're hurting me," Norah said again.

"And that matters to me? My dear lady, when you rejected me I knew something else had to be done." His eyes hardened as he inclined his face inches from hers. "If you do not sign the papers, something *will* happen to your children and your mother. You wouldn't want that now, would you?"

Her voice wavered and her knees wobbled. "Why is it that you are so set on having my land? You, Mr. Medina, and some other man in a neighboring town who mentioned it to Mr. Schreffler are all interested in it, but you'll hardly procure it with such crooked methods."

"You're an insolent woman. I'd say it's none of your business except I suppose it no longer matters. The Hammett farm will be mine soon. I had to convince Medina not to pursue it, but alas, I am a persuasive gentleman when I choose to be." A glower breached his mouth. "The reason I and everyone else want your land is because it's among the most fertile soil in this area. If your idiot husband would have agreed to my demands, we wouldn't be having this conversation. Of course, he was too mesmerized with Bridget to give thought to anything else." Payne paused and perused the fields. "It makes it all the better to know the wheat crop has started growing. Thank your hired hand you were supposed to fire for so diligently working the land. By his doing so, it will only add to my already immense holdings. My intention of owning all of the productive farmland in Cuyler Junction is finally coming to fruition."

Marcellus plucked the papers from Mr. Shreffler's hands, ripping the top one, and stormed toward Norah. He yanked her braid with such force she thought her neck would snap.

Payne freed her wrist and stepped aside.

Marcellus's face came within inches of hers. "You will sign them papers, and you will do it now." He unfettered his clamp on her.

Pain radiated from her head down her neck. Her breathing came in gasps, and her parched tongue cleaved to the roof of her mouth.

She would sign the papers to protect her family.

"May I read it first?" she whispered.

"Do as you wish. It won't make a bit of difference." Payne smoothed the unripped portion of the paper. "It states you are selling me the land. A lawyer prepared the document for us, and the second paper is Mr. Schreffler releasing you from your banknote. I, as the chivalrous man that I am, will assume your mortgage."

<hr>

Levi mounted his horse and rode to retrieve Norah. If all went well, he could double the potato crop next year.

Next year. He shook his head. So much had changed in such a short amount of time. Wasn't it just recently that he wasn't sure where his life would lead? Where he would go after leaving the only home he'd ever known?

Wasn't he convinced he'd never trust another woman after Criselda's decision to break their engagement? Yet here he was, not only trusting another woman, but falling in love with her.

He and Norah had grown closer in the past weeks. While she may never feel the same about him, he had come to care deeply for her.

Thunder roared overhead, and a breeze caused a miniature funnel in the dirt alongside the road. Spring rains were essential to a successful crop, although Levi much preferred the sunny warmth of an upcoming Idaho Territory summer.

As he neared the house, he noticed two buggies and a horse. Upon closer examination, three men, one of them being Payne Deaton, stood with Norah not far from the chicken coop.

Something wasn't right.

"Giddyap!" Eagle pressed forward, and Levi only slowed when he'd reached the house. He hastily dismounted and stalked toward the group. Norah's pallor and the way she trembled sent waves of worry up his spine. "Deaton, what brings you to the farm?"

"If it isn't the hired hand. Take care of him, Marcellus."

A tall, rotund man with a bushy beard, curly hair, and a bulbous nose fitting the description Norah had given of her attacker glowered at him. "Best you leave. This business don't concern you none."

"It concerns me when it concerns my employer." Levi brushed past him. "Norah, is everything all right?"

"I said it don't involve you!" The man shoved Levi hard in the shoulder.

"Levi, they are attempting to make me relinquish the farm to Payne."

"Is that true, Deaton?"

Before Payne could answer, Marcellus released a punch that hit Levi square in the jaw. Levi stumbled backwards before regaining his balance. Stars blinked in his vision as blood coated his tongue.

Levi prayed to stay alert and fight the confusion and dizziness from the blow. Teetering slightly, he braced himself in a solid stance, preparing for whatever else the man may have in mind.

Hadn't he been in a similar situation with Shipley? Only Shipley lacked muscle, strength, and size. The man Payne referred to as Marcellus may lack muscle, but he clearly possessed the latter two attributes.

Levi didn't want to get involved in an altercation. Not again. Hopefully this could be settled peacefully. "You three need to leave."

"Marcellus, earn your pay," retorted Payne.

Marcellus bent forward, and leading with his head, charged Levi, hitting with his shoulders and wrapping his arms around Levi's legs and lifting him before tackling him to the ground.

Levi's head hit the dirt below, and Marcellus's hands went around Levi's neck.

Marcellus had strength, but it was no match for the muscle Levi had built from years of hard work. Years of using the plow and hauling rock. He brought his fist up into Marcellus's throat. With a groan, the man released his hold on Levi. Without wasting a second, Levi then went for the man's eyes. Marcellus grappled at his face, offering an opportune time for Levi to throw his weight into Marcellus and shove him to the ground.

"Levi!" Norah's frantic cries sounded in his ears.

They tussled in a brawl, alternating the upper hand. Levi kneed Marcellus below the belt, then delivered a final hit that knocked the man unconscious.

Levi stood and braced his hands on his knees while he fought to catch his breath. He peered up to check on Norah just as Deaton fled to his buggy and drove away.

Norah rested a warm hand on his arm. "I was so worried."

He willed his body to cooperate as he attempted to stand up straight and reach for her hand. "I'm going to make sure Marcellus doesn't get away." He limped toward the barn, fetched two ropes, and secured the man's hands and ankles.

"Mr. Shreffler, would you be willing to fetch Sheriff Perez?"

The banker, whose cowering position near the clothesline had remained steadfast, took a sluggish step toward Levi. The color had drained from his face, leaving a sickly hue that rivaled the man's white hair. "I—yes, I can."

Norah ran to Levi and collapsed into his arms. He held her close and kissed the top of her head. He'd come so close to possibly losing her.

What if he'd not shown up when he did? What if Deaton and Marcellus decided to take their nefarious plans further if Norah hadn't obeyed their demands?

Thank You, Lord, for keeping her safe. For giving me the upper hand with Marcellus, and for watching over this woman who has come to mean so much to me.

Minutes slipped by with the only sound another roar of thunder and the only activity an occasional raindrop. Levi gently cupped her chin. "Are you all right?"

Moisture dampened her eyelashes. "Yes. Thank you, Levi."

He tenderly swiped away the tears. "Reckon it's all going to be fine now. Deaton and Marcellus will be brought to justice."

Chapter Eleven

Mama, Doc, and the children returned several minutes later. There was much she needed to tell her mother, but it would have to wait. She met them at the buggy, noting the questions in Mama's gaze.

Hazel peered around Enoch and Doc. "Ma, why is that man sleeping on the ground?"

"He's probably just tired is all," offered Enoch.

"Doc, would it be all right if Mama and the children stayed at your house for a few hours? Levi and I will retrieve them this evening. Mama, would that be amenable to you?"

Doc agreed, and Mama nodded.

"I'll explain everything this evening."

The doctor turned the buggy in the opposite direction and drove toward town. Hazel craned her neck the entire time they were in view, likely attempting to answer her own inquiry about the man "sleeping" on the ground.

Sheriff Perez arrived next with a wagon. "Mr. Shreffler told me what happened. From the sound of things, Marcellus will be spending some time in jail."

"And Payne?"

"Well, Mrs. Hammett, Payne will be doing more time in jail than even our friend, Marcellus. I've been watching him since I took the sheriff's position in Cuyler Junction. You're not the only one he's coerced or pressured into giving up their land. You're the first one who's endured Marcellus's abuse, but not the first to surrender to Payne's demands. I've spent considerable time with him, and the man is not who he pretends to be. Of course, all of this is up to the judge, but I reckon no one will have to worry about these two and their shenanigans again. What's more, I wouldn't doubt it one bit if Mrs. Deaton and her daughter hastened out of town on the next stagecoach."

Levi shook Sheriff Perez's hand. "Thank you, Sheriff. I did wonder why you and Deaton were smoking cigars in your office the day I came in to introduce myself."

"I figured as much. It wasn't because I enjoyed the man's company. Ever since a former resident of Cuyler Junction informed me he once owned a farm taken by Deaton, I knew it was cause for investigating. Glad I did. Would you mind assisting me with loading Marcellus into the wagon? This evening I'll pay a visit to the Deaton household."

Norah thanked the Lord once again for His Providence in keeping her and Levi safe and that the children and Mama were gone when Payne and Marcellus paid their visit.

Then Levi held her in his arms, his hand gently on her back. He rested his chin on her head, and Norah closed her eyes and relished the warmth and safety.

He took a step back and took her hand in his. "There's something I need to tell you." His brow furrowed, and he scrubbed a free hand over his face. "I hope you won't think less of me, but I reckon you should know the truth." A haunted expression filled his countenance.

Impending dread tied her stomach in knots. "I'm sure I won't think less of you."

"Norah..." he cleared his throat. "I was in jail before I came to Cuyler Junction."

"In jail?"

"Yes."

Tears smarted her eyes. Being in jail could only mean one thing, and she refused to believe Levi was an outlaw. Not this man who'd risked his own life to protect her. Not the man who was largely responsible for the change in Enoch. Not the man who sat beside her in church each Sunday, made it possible for the farm's first successful crop, and who traded his labor for the wood to fix her porch.

Not the man she'd grown to love.

"I'd rather not know," she whispered.

He gently rubbed a calloused thumb on her cheek, and she squeezed her eyes shut.

"You need to know, Norah. I don't want there to be any secrets between us."

Her eyes fluttered open, and she witnessed the grief in the depth of Levi's gaze. "All right."

"You once asked me why I didn't miss working for my pa. I didn't miss working for him because he never liked me. All during my growing-up years, he had no good words to say to me. I learned to keep to myself and avoid time with him. My younger brother, Jay, and I moved into the bunkhouse on a man named Shipley's property. Shipley was also our employer, and my parents rented a cabin from him on the farm where all three of us men worked. Pa was a stern man, and Ma never showed much affection either. To me, anyway. Jay had earned their love, but for me, such an endearment from them wasn't possible. Believe me, I did try. Tried my hardest to win their love. To do everything Pa wanted me to. For him, I was merely a workhorse and a means to stay working Shipley's farm."

"I'm so sorry. I had no idea."

"It's not something I share." He shrugged. "For the longest time, I believed my Heavenly Father was just like my earthly one. Cold, indifferent, and ready to mete out punishment whenever I made a mistake, whether accidental or intentional. A man named Elmer whom I met on my way here taught me otherwise. In the three days I spent with him, I learned more about the Bible and God's Word than I'd ever known. He answered all my questions and offered advice. Elmer and I parted ways when he went to Nevada to see his family, and I continued my search in for a town where I could find employment."

Norah rested her hand on his arm. "Were it not for you telling me otherwise, I would never have guessed you didn't have a godly father given the way you've taken to Enoch and mentored him."

"I made up my mind long ago I'd never be like my own pa." He released a heavy sigh. "Mr. Shipley's wife rarely left their home. I always figured it was because it was the nicest home in our town, much fancier than anything I'd ever seen before. But the truth of the matter was, Mr. Shipley was taking out his frustrations on her. With his fists."

Norah gasped. "Oh, the poor woman." While Douglas had been a selfish and unfaithful husband, he'd never laid a hand on her or the children. For that she was grateful.

"One day, I watched as her husband used his fists on her. He'd been drinking at the saloon, and when he came home, he yelled at her for not having supper ready. I witnessed it all and knew I couldn't stand idly by while a man abused his wife. I stepped in, showed Shipley how it felt to be hit, and told his wife to go to town to a friend's house."

"Did she?"

"She did not. She went into her own house after apologizing to her husband for angering him. Meanwhile, Shipley had me arrested and his wife refused to admit he was abusing her. She instead told the sheriff she fell down the stairs and that was the cause for her bruises."

Norah's stomach lurched, and bile rose in her throat. How could anyone harm someone—especially someone they vowed to love—in such a horrible way? "And you spent time in jail for your brawl with Mr. Shipley?"

"I did. Now, I rarely went to church. My pa didn't care about the Lord, and Ma, well, she would pray every now and again and she had a Bible, but we didn't know the reverend as more than an acquaintance. I have no idea what he thought of the entire situation, but in the small town—about half the size or less than Cuyler Junction—everyone thought ill of me for what I'd done. They saw me as a ruffian who didn't agree with my employer, so I attacked him. But no one cared about the truth. Not my parents, not Jay, and not Criselda."

"Criselda?"

Levi's shoulders slumped. "Two days before the Shipley incident, I proposed to her. We'd courted for about six months, and I truly believed she was the one for me. Now I know otherwise. I doubt I ever really loved her. The thought of maybe starting my own family was a dream of mine, and a way to escape the family I'd been born into."

"Did Criselda break off the engagement?"

"She did. While I was in jail, she paid me a visit and said she no longer wanted anything to do with me."

Norah squeezed his arm. "I'm so sorry, Levi."

"I vowed never to fall in love again and never to trust anyone again. People weren't trustworthy, not even my parents, and for sure not the woman I thought I loved."

"Not everyone is like that, but I do understand. I felt the same way after what Douglas did."

"Douglas was a fool to ever walk away from you."

Norah allowed his words to sink deep within her heart. "Thank you."

"I was in jail for a week until Mrs. Shipley came forward and told the sheriff the truth. That her husband was beating her and that she planned to leave and return to her family back East. Thankfully, Shipley didn't attempt to stop her. I was released, but my father disowned me, and I left town the same day without ever looking back. Before I left, I never would have prayed for God's will in my life. But after talking with Elmer and surrendering my life to Jesus, I realized God knows what's better for me much more than I do."

She recalled how it had taken her a significant amount of time to trust that the Lord could truly take care of her worries as well. "Thank you for sharing that with me, Levi."

"Do you think less of me?"

"Not at all. I saw how you reacted when you learned Marcellus attacked me the first time and then how you came to my aid today."

"Thank you for listening and for believing me." Levi put an arm around her, and she leaned her head against his shoulder. He tenderly rubbed her arm and brushed a gentle kiss on her forehead.

A warmth zipped through her and her heart leapt against her chest at his touch.

"Norah?"

"Yes?" Her voice barely emerged as a whisper.

Levi kissed the top of her nose. "Will you do me the honor of courting you?"

"Yes."

His fingertip traced her bottom lip. "May I kiss you?"

Her nod gave him the permission he needed and she closed her eyes as his lips found hers. She fell into his embrace, savoring the warmth.

The smell of rain filled the air, and the crisp newness reminded Norah of the new life she would begin with Levi in their courtship, and hopefully, if the Lord willed, someday marriage.

Epilogue

June, 1881

LEVI TOOK NORAH'S HAND in his, and they walked along the road adjacent to the fields of the Callahan farm. Enoch and Hazel joined them with Mayflower, who periodically turned, barked, wagged her tail, then bounded forward again.

Enoch threw a bone, and Mayflower retrieved it and returned it to her owner.

"Look, Pa. I taught Mayflower how to fetch and carry." The boy wrestled the bone from Mayflower, who yipped at his feet, begging to play the game again.

Levi ruffled Enoch's hair. "Good job, son."

Enoch beamed. "And that's not all. I'm gonna teach her other tricks too."

Hazel planted her hands on her hips and focused her attention on her brother. "I know a trick we can teach her. Pa, can you build her a special chair so she can sit at the table with us for supper? I'm gonna show her how to hold a fork."

"Oh, poppycock, Hazel. Dogs can't hold forks." Enoch shook his head and rolled his eyes.

"Mayflower can. She's a smart dog. So, Pa, can you build her a special chair? Then I could help her put her paws on the table. I bet I could even teach her how to pray before the meal." Hazel, never one for a lack of words, prattled on as if she had planned beforehand every detail.

Levi chuckled. "Not sure I can build her a special chair. Besides, your ma may not cotton to the idea of a dog sitting at the table and eating a meal with us."

"Your pa is right. As delightful as Mayflower is, I don't anticipate her joining us at the table or eating with a fork anytime soon. However..." Norah tapped her chin. "I bet you could teach her how to sit and beg for a treat."

Enoch thumbed his chest. "I can teach her that." He threw the bone again, and Mayflower darted toward it.

Levi stopped then and took in the view of the farm from where they stood. Wheat and potatoes in one direction, the house, barn, corral, and bunkhouse in the other.

He was a blessed man.

Levi wrapped his arms around Norah and kissed the top of her head. She snuggled into his arms, and he thanked the Lord for His Providence.

Last winter, he and Norah married, exactly one month after Bess and Doc. The bountiful harvest allowed them to pay on the banknote as well as the tool loan, and Levi hired a hand to assist him and Enoch with the crops.

His hands rested on Norah's belly, which housed their new little one for six more months. His wife turned around then and faced him, her beauty stealing his breath as it always did.

"I love you, Levi Callahan."

"And I love you, Norah Callahan."

She lifted her chin, and he brushed a kiss on her forehead before claiming her lips with his.

And Levi vowed to love this woman God had blessed him with forever.

Love's New Beginnings

Sneak Peek

USUALLY SHE WAS A calm and mild-mannered young woman.

Usually.

But not today.

Today, decorum was the last thing on her mind.

Lydie Beauchamp stalked down the dusty streets of Prune Creek, her skirt swishing against her ankles.

Both Aunt Fern and Aunt Myrtle would have her hide and then some if they knew what she was about to do. *"So uncharacteristic of you, child,"* Aunt Fern would say.

"You really ought to remember the proper way to handle disputes," Aunt Myrtle would admonish.

Even with the thoughts of how her aunts might respond *if* they found out, Lydie's fury was about to spring to life.

Lydie passed the barber shop, livery, blacksmith, and the church that doubled as a schoolhouse. She marched past the bank, saloon, and post office until she reached the mercantile, where *he* stood loading items into his saddlebag.

She wished she were spunky like Aunt Myrtle, rather than quiet and reserved.

*Although...*quiet and reserved might not be the words *he* would use to describe her once she unleashed her thoughts about the whole ordeal.

"Miss Beauchamp, of what do I owe the pleasure?" The man in his forties with a black handlebar mustache removed his hat, revealing a large balding spot in his otherwise graying black hair.

"You know exactly why I'm here, Mr. Wilkins." Lydie did her best to raise her voice, but it still came out squeaky like that of a young child. She would need to work on that if she was ever going to be a teacher and deal with wayward pupils.

Mr. Wilkins smirked. "Now, now, young lady. You know full well it wasn't ever going to work between your aunt and me."

"But Aunt Fern moved here to the Wyoming Territory just so the two of you could marry. And now you have called off the wedding two days before the event." She placed her hands on her hips and did her best to glower.

Apparently, it was not very convincing because Mr. Wilkins only laughed.

"South Pass City is calling me." He held a hand to his right ear. "That precious thing called gold is calling me. Prune Creek and being married and settling down with Fern are not."

Lydie had heard of South Pass City and the gold that was to be found in the town a great distance from Prune Creek. But she'd never anticipated that Aunt Fern's intended would be drawn into the lure of hunting for it.

Not that she knew Mr. Wilkins well. To the contrary, she'd only met him a month ago when she and her aunts moved from Minnesota to the wilds of the Wyoming Territory.

"You made a vow to marry Aunt Fern. An honorable man never goes back on his word." Why did her voice sound so tinny? She cleared her throat and tried again. "You promised to marry her, settle down with her, and make a life with her in Prune Creek."

Mr. Wilkins shook his head. "She must have misunderstood. Look, Miss Beauchamp, I have a lot of riding ahead of me if I want to make some headway before nightfall. Sorry you're upset and all about Fern, but this is the way it is. She'll find someone else."

But Lydie had an inkling Aunt Fern would never find someone else, for her heart was broken beyond repair.

"But, Mr. Wilkins…"

"No two ways about it, Miss Beauchamp. I'm not staying in Prune Creek and I'm not marrying Fern." He swung a leg over the horse and settled into the saddle.

And then that despicable man rode off heading south.

Her eyes smarted with tears. Not because she had failed at convincing Mr. Wilkins to stay and marry Aunt Fern, but because he had hurt someone Lydie cared about more than life itself.

The thundering sound of the stagecoach rumbling down the road toward town shifted Lydie's focus, and she stepped up onto the boardwalk. She closed her eyes as a plume of dust engulfed the air.

Lord, please help Aunt Fern. Help her heart to heal.

Lydie sighed and began her walk toward home before the aunts realized she'd disappeared.

Home.

They'd left behind all they had in Minnesota to chase Aunt Fern's dreams. While they hadn't many possessions at their former residence, they *did* have a home in which to reside, and the aunts had taken in mending and washing to support themselves. Now, here in the Wild West where outlaws perched on every corner, horse thieves and cattle rustlers were the norm, and nothing refined or cultured existed in the dusty town, their futures appeared bleak.

So much for new beginnings.

They couldn't return to Minnesota, for there was nothing left for them there. No family and no home. Aunt Fern, having so excitedly shared the news with their church friends about marrying a handsome cowboy in the Wild West, would never return to announce her failure.

The single women had swooned at Aunt Fern's exuberance. Aunt Myrtle, who could be quite contrary, supported Aunt Fern to the fullest and agreed the move was best for them all. Lydie figured deep down inside, Aunt Myrtle was a romantic at heart, just like her sister.

Lydie sighed. How could they support themselves here? She'd applied for the teaching position at the school to no avail. According to rumors perpetuated by the mercantile owner's wife, Miss Owsten planned to teach until she was ninety-nine. Lydie obviously couldn't wait that long.

The aunts had taken in some mending, but it apparently wasn't a priority here to have clothing in satisfactory condition. Men appreciated the missing buttons on their worn and smelly old shirts. And while men outnumbered the women by a ratio of six to one, none of them were suitable beaus for either of the aunts.

Lydie stepped into the post office. Perhaps one of their Minnesota friends had written to inquire as to their well-being. After all, the aunts had declared their move to be one of excitement and adventure. The things written about in dime novels.

"Hello, Miss Beauchamp. How did you know I had a letter for you?" The post office clerk, a man whose name she couldn't recall offhand, reached into one of the slots to retrieve the correspondence.

"You mean for the aunts?"

"No, this one is addressed to you." The clerk handed her the letter.

Lydie inhaled a sharp breath. Could it be?

Her name, in scrawled and slanted penmanship, peered up at her.

She closed her eyes, breathed a prayer, and released the breath she'd been holding. She couldn't open it. Couldn't. So much depended on the words penned inside.

"Might you open this for me?" Lydie slightly opened one eye and attempted to hand the letter to the clerk.

"Me?" the postal clerk recoiled. "But it is addressed to you." He shook his head. "No, miss, you best open it."

Lydie could just toss the letter in the fireplace tonight and not give it another thought.

Oh, but she would give it another thought. And dwell on it for days, pondering what might have been. Deliberating the words written on the page, neatly tucked inside the envelope.

Lord, may Your will be done.

That was a difficult prayer, for Lydie's desire could quite possibly be vastly different than the Lord's plans for her.

Five minutes later, she was on the boardwalk again, still clutching the envelope. A crinkle along the edges testified to her firm, albeit nervous, grasp on it. Finally, she opened the flap, daring herself to scan the words upon the page.

Dear Miss Beauchamp,

I trust this finds you doing well.

I am pleased to announce that you have been chosen for the teaching position in Willow Falls. Room and board and a small stipend will be provided, and the first day of school will commence on the second Monday in September.

Please respond posthaste if you are still interested.
Sincerely,
Mr. Morton
School Board Chairman

Lydie's heart raced, and she re-read the letter five more times. She'd never met the school board chairman, and she'd never been to Willow Falls, a town over the mountain from Prune Creek. But soon she would be the new teacher, and not only the new teacher, but the very *first* teacher.

She held a hand to her bosom. Could she teach? Could she inspire and mold young minds? Could she succeed at this dream of a new beginning in her life? Would the couple with whom she would stay be charitable? Would the kindly townsfolk take pity and give her a second chance if she failed in her attempts?

Would she be able to be away from the aunts?

The latter concerned her the most.

Fear, apprehension, and worry niggled their way into Lydie's heart. Perhaps deciding to be a teacher was not the calling God had placed on her life. Perhaps the letter was intended for someone else.

But sure enough, when she unfolded the stationery and peeked again at the salutation, her name was there amongst the somewhat-messy and overly-slanted penmanship.

There was another matter which demanded her full attention. Whether she should accept the teaching position in Willow Falls or remain in Prune Creek depended on a critical happenstance. She must find a way for the aunts to support themselves, either that or bring them along with her to Willow Falls.

A new adventure it would be if they all three moved once again to a new town. Aunt Myrtle and Aunt Fern thrived on change. Lydie did not. But it would be a doable adventure if she didn't have to do it alone. Quite possibly, there would be a job for them mending and sewing in Willow Falls, although if this was the first time a school teacher was to be hired, the town was likely smaller than Prune Creek. That posed the problem of job opportunities.

Moments later, she returned home, the letter carefully hidden in her bodice. The aunts mustn't know of the teaching position, for if they did, they would encourage her to accept without delay. They'd always been supportive of her dreams and had taken such good care of her in all these years after her parents died.

No, she wouldn't tell them about the acceptance until she had a plan in place. Perhaps she wouldn't even accept the offer to be the first teacher in Willow Falls after all.

Lydie snuck past the aunts and into her meager portion of the log cabin, a minuscule area behind a curtain that provided just enough room for a bed and a bureau. She then proceeded to pace. Three steps to the curtain, three steps to the bed. Then all over again.

"Child, you are about to wear a hole in the floor." Aunt Myrtle's voice rose above the clomp-clomp of Lydie's boots.

"And I see your feet going this way and that," added Aunt Fern, her voice teary. "What has you so jittery and overwrought?"

If only you knew, my dear aunts.

Aunt Myrtle spoke again. "Come out here and have something to eat. I need your help with Aunt Fern."

Lydie wondered what the problem may be with Aunt Fern, but surmised it must have to do with Mr. Wilkins's brash behavior. She tucked the letter inside her bureau beneath her Sunday dress, pushed the curtain aside, and stepped into the humble common area.

Aunt Myrtle sliced a piece of bread. "Care for a sandwich for the noonday meal?" she asked.

A sandwich sounded delicious, although who could eat at a time like this when the very future of three lives teetered on one person's choice? Yet her stomach rumbled, reminding her she hadn't eaten since early that morning. "Yes, thank you."

"Now, Lydie, remind Aunt Fern that nourishment is necessary for survival."

Lydie placed an arm around Aunt Fern. "You know what Aunt Myrtle is saying is true."

"Are you taking sides?" Aunt Fern dabbed at her eyes with a doily.

"Did you mean to wipe your eyes with the doily?" Lydie handed her aunt the checkered handkerchief that rested on the table next to the lace doily.

"Dear me, no." That caused another round of sobs, and Lydie regretted her attempts at making light of the situation. She drew Aunt Fern to her, placed her chin on her aunt's head, and did her best to comfort her.

Aunt Myrtle stood with her hands on her hips. "Of course Lydie is taking sides. I'm right in this matter. And *most* matters."

Lydie held her tongue. Aunt Myrtle was a spirited one and most definitely *not* right in most matters. Even so, she cared deeply for her younger sister and only wanted what was best for her.

"Why did we come all this way and leave everything behind? I feel so distraught at the thought of upending our lives like I did. Will you both ever find it in your hearts to forgive me?"

"You're already forgiven, now quit with the nonsense," admonished Aunt Myrtle.

Lydie patted Aunt Fern's arm. "Of course, we forgive you. How were you to know that despicable dolt would cause such an upheaval of the heart?"

"Upheaval of the heart?" Aunt Fern peered up at Lydie through teary eyes. "Wherever did you come up with that phrase, child?"

Lydie loved to read, so it could have been from one of the few novels they owned that she'd recently re-read for the fiftieth time. Or it could have been from her own mind. Not that she would admit it to anyone, but she was a bit on the romantic side. But romance was not something she could discuss at this moment, especially not with Aunt Fern's broken heart. "Not quite sure, Aunt Fern, but I do know that you are such a dear, and if you don't receive proper nourishment, you'll waste away to skin and bones and succumb to an early death. Aunt Myrtle and I would forever be in a state of melancholy without you here."

Even to her own ears, Lydie sounded rather dramatic, and she didn't think of herself as the dramatic type. More like a shy and reserved woman with plentiful inner contemplations. But if she had to be lively in her delivery in order to persuade Aunt Fern to eat, then she would do so.

"It's only been today that I've not eaten. Surely I won't succumb to an early death quite so soon." Aunt Fern pursed her lips. "You know it's unbecoming of you two to conspire against me."

Aunt Myrtle put a ham sandwich in front of her sister. "But ally ourselves together, we must. If you'll recall, dear sister, you and Lydie did the very same thing to me that time at the county fair."

Lydie and Aunt Fern shared a knowing glance. Aunt Myrtle was gifted in many ways, but her attention to detail, especially when it came to baking, left much to be desired. The judges at the fair thought so as well when they tasted the sugarless blueberry pie Aunt Myrtle entered.

"True," said Aunt Fern. "But that was because that blueberry pie *was* awful. Who forgets to add sugar to a recipe?" She puckered her lips in a sour expression as if tasting the tart pie all over again. Unfortunately, they'd eaten far too much of it since there had been plenty of the pie left over after the judging.

Aunt Myrtle's brows perched low into a frown. "Bringing up the past is not conducive to this discussion."

"Alas, we shan't talk about that wretched blueberry pie and worsen this difficult time in my life." Aunt Fern sniffled and daintily blew her nose in, thankfully, the handkerchief and not the lace doily.

Perhaps a licorice whip would ease some of Aunt Fern's melancholy. Lydie did have a penny saved up for a special purpose. After the noonday meal, she'd walk to the mercantile and purchase one of her aunt's favorite candies. And while she was there, Lydie would inquire as to whether there was a job opening for one or both of her aunts at the mercantile.

If that didn't work, she'd invite them both to follow her to Willow Falls.

If she accepted the position.

If you want to be among the first to hear about
the next release, sign up for Penny's newsletter
at www.pennyzeller.com You will receive book and
writing updates, encouragement, notification of current
giveaways, occasional freebies, and special offers. Plus,
you'll receive *An Unexpected Arrival*, a Wyoming Sunrise
novelette, for free.

AUTHOR'S NOTE

Dear Reader,

Thank you for once again journeying with me to the late 1800s. As you've probably ascertained, the beautiful state of Idaho is one of my favorite settings. When the idea of this story first came to me, I knew I wanted to create two broken people who'd been hurt deeply by others. Such hurt made trust a challenge, but both had faith in knowing that God was One they *could* trust.

Characters are always a delight to create. Learning the traits of main characters and their strengths and weaknesses and then weaving that together into the story is one of my favorite parts about writing a book. Of course, a book couldn't be a book without strong secondary characters. Mama, Hazel, Enoch, Doc, Elmer, Audney, and Mrs. Winrow served that purpose, and I especially enjoyed writing Hazel's and Enoch's characters.

In *Levi's Vow*, I did touch on the topics of infidelity, divorce, and spousal abuse. Unfortunately, Mrs. Shipley did blame herself at first after being abused by her husband. Thankfully, she removed herself from the danger and sought refuge with family in a distant state. Spousal abuse and domestic violence continue to be a serious problem in our country. At the time of publication of this book, according to the CDC, "about 1 in 3 women and about 1 in 4 men report having experienced severe physical violence from an intimate partner in their lifetime." If you or someone you love is a victim of domestic violence, please call 1-800-799-SAFE (7233).

Thank you for taking the time to read *Levi's Vow*. I am so appreciative of my readers.

Until next time, happy reading!

Blessings,

Penny

Acknowledgments

To my family. I can never thank you enough for your encouragement, support, and patience as I put words to paper. I'm so grateful for you.

Thank you my husband, Lon, a former Idaho farm boy, for helping me learn the logistics about growing wheat and potatoes.

To my Penny's Peeps Street Team and my launch team members. Thank you for spreading the word about my books. I appreciate your encouragement and support.

To my beta readers. You are the ones who see my project at its beginning stages. Thank you for all of your wonderful suggestions.

To Marie Concannon for continually sharing her knowledge of all things historical.

To my readers. May God bless and guide you as you grow in your walk with Him.

And, most importantly, thank you to my Lord and Savior, Jesus Christ. It is my deepest desire to glorify You with my writing and help bring others to a knowledge of Your saving grace.

About the Author

Penny Zeller is known for her heartfelt stories of faith-filled happily ever afters and her passion to impact lives for Christ through fiction. Her books feature tender romance, steady doses of humor, and memorable characters that stay with you long after the last page.

While she has had a love for writing since childhood, Penny began her adult writing career penning articles for national and regional publications on a wide variety of topics. Today Penny is a multi-published author of over three dozen books and is also a fitness instructor, loves the outdoors, and is a flower gardening addict. In her spare time, she enjoys camping, hiking, kayaking, biking, birdwatching, reading, running, and playing volleyball.

Penny resides with her husband and two daughters in small-town America and loves to connect with her readers at her website at www.pennyzeller.com. All of her socials can be found at https://linktr.ee/pennyzeller.

MONTANA HEARTS

Hilltop Series

HOLLOW CREEK

WYOMING SUNRISE

Love in Cloverdale Falls

Christian Rom-Coms
with Heart and Humor

CONTEMPORARY ROMANCES

STANDALONE

CHOKECHERRY HEIGHTS SERIES

Christian Romantic Suspense

Close Proximity

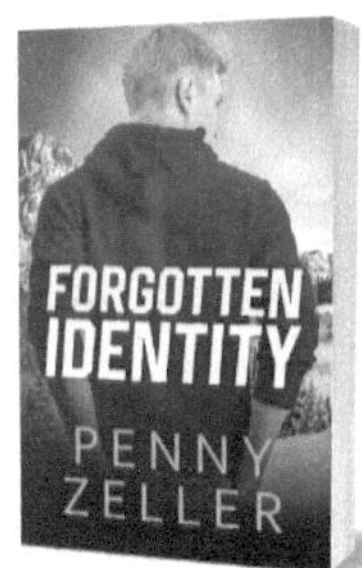

Mountain Justice